Map of The Comanche Empire approx. 1850

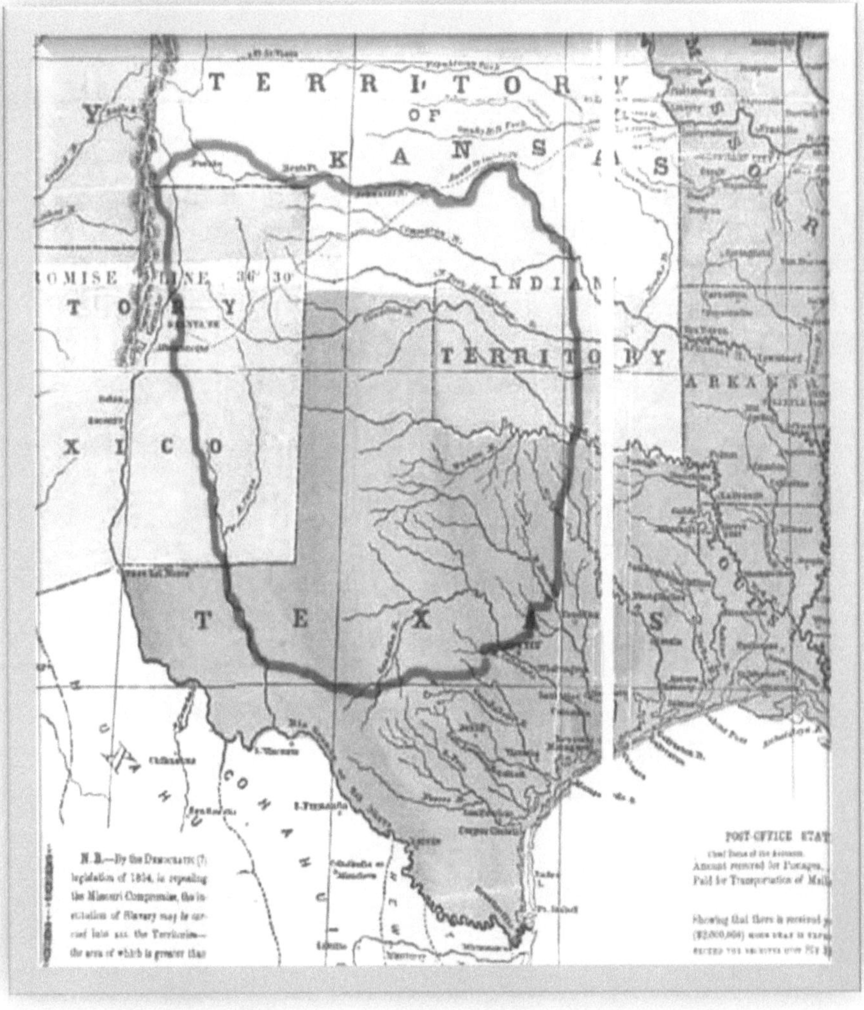

Based on Reynolds's Political Map of the United States 1856 –
from Library of Congress collection

Printed in the United States of America

First Printing, 2017

ISBN 0692860959

Evans-Bronstein Publishing

Dedication:

I dedicate this work to my dear wife Ariella and my children, Ayelet, Yael, Shaya, Shlomo, Meir, and Lilly.
Also to my son Mickey, may your memory be a blessing.

"Although we are not all born a Comanche, if the high plain is in your blood, you can become one..." - Charlie Bird

Contents

Prologue

A piercing wind swept the creek bank, snapping the teepee flaps. The storm, locally known as a Blue Norther, was intense for December. Temperatures had fallen precipitously—thirty degrees in the last hour—and the snow seemed to come from every direction, blasting the trees with an incredible intensity.

Within one of the tents, a mother tenderly gathered her two-year-old daughter into her arms and pressed the toddler close against the cold. She gently stroked the little girl's hair and glanced nervously at the opening to her home. Small flakes of snow pushed their way inside and whirled about in the fire-warmed air before vanishing as they touched the earthen floor.

Her twelve-year-old son slept peacefully on a buffalo skin next to the fire. In a matter of weeks, the boy would be old enough to join the hunting and raiding parties.

Something was not right. Her husband, the great chief, should have been back by now. Worrying that he and her oldest son might be trapped somewhere out on the plains kept her from sleep. Had they found shelter in time? The appearance of this storm had been so sudden!

Without warning, from out in the dark line of trees that bordered the creek, the chief's wife heard a loud popping sound. It was the report of a rifle.

The deep-throated yell of soldiers soon pierced the howling blizzard, followed immediately by screams from the surprised women and children. More shots rang out, mixing with the cries of the wounded and dying.

The young boy woke with a start, sprang to his feet and grabbed his own rifle, and then made for the entrance.

His mother reached out, arresting his departure with a grip made strong with fear.

"Do not fight! Now is the time to flee!"

"Mother, I must defend our people! The other men are away hunting!"

"If you do, I fear you will never return! I have a feeling!"

The young man smiled and gently caressed his mother's cheek. *"I shall return. Worry not!"*

Reluctantly, his mother released him. Stifling a cry, she watched as the boy rushed from the tent with a warrior's yell.

The following day, Chief Nocona stood at the edge of the tribal encampment and surveyed the wreckage of his people. Still-smoldering scars blackened the snow, marking where the teepees had once stood. The sun was bright now, shining through the beeches that lined the creek.

With tears in his eyes, he bent over a small blanket. It was empty now but had once held a lovely child, a flower of the prairie. She was gone along with her mother, nowhere to be found. Several lifeless forms lay huddled in varying positions of agony. The brutes had not even had the decency to bury the dead.

His son, Quanah, was busy with the other warriors in identifying those whose spirits had departed to the next world. The young warrior cried out when he turned over one of the bodies. He thrust his fist to his mouth in anguish and ran to his father.

"Enapay is dead!"

"I feared as much. Your brother would never run! Wrap him in a buffalo hide and begin with the graves for our people." Then, the great warrior's shoulders sagged and he sank down on a log. He buried his face in his hands and sobbed uncontrollably. Everything he'd had when he'd left the morning before was gone! How would he continue on? What was left? Who would replace the warriors lost?

The great chief's bones ached. The end was near. Soon enough Quanah would be leader. Was he equal to the task?

The Chief

The Man

He hated the cane. It was an impediment to movement and more than that, it was a testament to his lessening influence. Whether due to age or the changing times, it mattered not. At one point, he had commanded an army, a huge tribe of warriors with the ability to raid a fort or village over fifteen hundred miles away and return in a matter of days, laden with plunder and scalps.

Those days had long since passed, however. Now, if he were lucky, he might hobble into an audience with an assistant of the great chief in Washington and gain a small concession to feed his people.

Thirty years ago, the Comanches were center stage on the national agenda. Now, in the advanced year of 1911, they were relegated to a curiosity. They were perhaps fodder for the new moving pictures industry, but even then, they were nothing more substantial than a sideshow.

Today was different and less depressing. Quanah was expecting a visitor. Not any guest, but a fellow warrior. A brother, in fact.

The chief had shared adventures, trials, tragedies, and triumphs with this man, and their years apart had not made them strangers. Whenever Quanah's thoughts traveled back to those last days on the warpath, Charlie Bird was indelibly intertwined with those memories.

The daring escapes and close calls, the carefully planned battles and raids, all formed a collage of the most intricate emotional tapestry. When one faces danger and adventures with another, the bond formed is unbreakable.

The ensuing years after the surrender following the Red River war had been prosperous for Quanah. He had gained the favor of the white man as the last chief of the Comanche and he had leveraged that influence to help his people. Those tribe members had all contributed to the great Star House with its two-story porch and immense white stars on the roof that shone for miles across the reservation. "This," they would say, "is a house fit for a chief!"

Quanah did not live in lazy luxury, but rather used the home to entertain important guests, all the while angling for a better future for his people, squeezed through handshakes and oozing smiles from his wealthy and influential guests.

He had adopted some of the white man's ways, but not all of them. He would never practice their religion. He had his own ideas about the creator and would stick to them, come what may.

Another concession he would never make was having a single wife. It didn't make sense to him. So, he had filled his Star House with wives and children and then later, grandchildren and even great grandchildren. They ran about the house, bumping into the furniture and generally spreading joy wherever they were.

Just now, one of his grandchildren was practicing with a lance in the front yard, puncturing a bale of hay with a mighty thrust. Quanah smiled ruefully to himself at the thought that now, this was just a game. Years ago, it was survival.

The Letter

The beautiful afternoon sun bathed the front porch in a bright, golden light. Orange trees dotted the rolling hills of the Bird Estate as children played in the yard.

Rebecca surveyed the scene from the door to her spacious house with equanimity. Life had been good and the family had prospered, with the name Bird Oranges becoming a household term in Southern California. She had been part and parcel of the success, encouraging her husband to grow their land holdings and push for better prices for the produce.

Raising the children had been her greatest accomplishment as far as she was concerned. Her oldest grandchild was nearing his twentieth year and was the very picture of his father. At the same age her husband had been a Comanche warrior who had raided white settlements and settled scores in blood. His past had left a hard edge that, while not violent, caused Charlie to be somewhat distant and brooding at times. Those personality traits were totally absent in her forty year old son and myriad of grandchildren.

The other grandchildren, five girls and two boys, were remarkable for their fine appearance and intelligence. They did however lack the leadership qualities she saw in her eldest grandson. There was something special about him and she was sure, with the Good Lord's help, that he would one day become a great man.

Two strong hands gripped her shoulders from behind.

"Rebecca dear, what are you thinking about?" Charlie asked.

She turned to regard his still handsome face.

"Of the grandchildren. Where life will lead them and what they will become. You know, the usual musings of a grandmother."

"Well, I must say, you are incredible. The family is well cared for and happy."

She threw her arms around her husband's neck and smiled.

"And we can't forget their excellent grandfather!"

"Ah! I'm not much. I'm around to pick the oranges is all!"

"No! You and I both know that is not true! The grandchildren adore you and you teach them so much! They've learned to ride, to farm, and even about business from you. It's no small feat that they are all excelling in school and the boy is headed to college and it's not all my doing."

"OK, perhaps I'll accept the compliment."

Then the smile faded from his face and his gaze left hers for the distant fields.

Rebecca, always a quick study of human emotion, asked pleadingly, "Charlie, what troubles you? You were here one moment and off in the distance the next."

"It is nothing. I was just thinking of my brother. He wrote to me. I received his letter by the post today. He says he is sick and wishes to see me again, perhaps for the last time."

Her face fell at the news. She knew how much Charlie's brother meant to him. "Well then, you must go," she said, matter of factly. Then she continued, " We will all go. It's important for everyone to see the great chief before it is too late."

"Indeed we will. Of course, there's more of the usual from the government, he writes. They have held back food and supplies and instead given it to contractors to distribute. These villains are not giving it to the people but keeping it for themselves. Quanah fears that many will die this winter."

"Dear, the situation is different now. There has not been war for 30 years and the government has made promises to protect the

Indians. It is in the best interests of the politicians to make sure they keep their word. Isnt it?"

"The Natives have fallen out of the public's view. There are so many more pressing matters in people's minds. The Comanche, the Kiowa, the Sioux and the Cheyenne, they mean little anymore."

"But Charlie... if that's true, then you must speak to your connections in Washington!"

"I was thinking the very same thing. I will wire the good senator immediately to see what can be done."

Rebecca thought about what all this meant for a moment and then stated matter-of-factly, "G-d will be with you, Charlie!"

Together Again

Quanah looked west toward the setting sun. A board creaked and Charlie stepped lightly onto the porch. At the sound, the great chief rose creakily to his feet and turned to greet his guest, the wealthy philanthropist, Charlie Bird. His wife, Rebecca, soon joined them on the porch.

"Ah, Charlie!" he spoke in his native dialect. "Time has been kind to you." Switching to English he added, "And Rebecca, you look as lovely as ever!"

Rebecca smiled at the compliment. This man had lost none of his charm.

Charlie spoke as he stepped forward to embrace Quanah, "And time has been kind to you too, brother!"

"Yes, I suppose I don't look a day older than the hills!" he joked, punching the younger man's arm playfully.

"Some things never change! How do you feel?"

"Tired and achy. It is, I fear, the lot for all of us one time or another, although I think maybe never for you! You look the same as when we left Bad Hand screaming between the mountains."

"Indeed! I feel my age too oft times! Ha! Do you remember the look on his face? A cross between a startled buffalo and a trapped cougar!"

Charlie burst out in sustained laughter and was soon joined by the chief.

Children gathered around the pair to see what was making the two old men laugh, one a lithe figure, and the other, his huge frame bent with age, dressed as a country gentleman.

"What makes you laugh, grandfather?" one of the braver members of the group inquired.

"We share memories of our times past! Do you not recognize my brother, Charlie Bird?"

Most of them nodded in affirmation.

"Yes, we certainly did have some good times!" Then, turning to the children, Charlie asked, "Would you all like to hear some of the stories?"

The youngsters heads bobbed up and down as they jumped about, excited to have a chance to hear all about the adventures of their famous elders firsthand.

The two warriors sat down on the wooden porch chairs and glanced at each other to see who should start first. Soon enough though, the pair would begin telling the tales with gusto, sometimes talking over the other's words in excitement of being the first to tell a harrowing adventure or a humorous anecdote.

The Parker Massacre

One moment the fields were clear and the next they were covered with Indians, more than she could count.

Minutes earlier, Rachel Plummer had walked into the fields, already hot in the May sun, to bring water to her husband, Luther. He graciously accepted the drink and wiped his brow.

"That is certainly better. It's been getting awfully hot out here, but you can see how the crops are getting on!"

Luther placed an arm around his wife and looked with pride on the new plot of land he had been working. In a few months they'd have their second child and build a cabin adjacent to the fields they called their own. The future seemed bright for the Plummer family.

The Comanche and their allies had other plans. It seems the Parkers, who had established the fort and invited their kinfolk to populate the place, had been hosting Texas Rangers which the Indians found detestable. John Parker, the elder, an old Indian hunter and negotiator himself, had also made various treaties with the neighboring natives. He thought that when one tribe accepted peace, it meant they all had. John Parker had been wrong. He had left out the most important bands of all, not even contacting them. In their eyes, this was considered an insult not to be taken lightly. That was why they came that day to wipe Fort Parker from the map.

A choked scream was brought forth by Rachel as she saw the vast number of shirtless, painted warriors approach the stockade.

Luther pushed her towards the fort. "Hurry for the safety of the walls!" he exhorted her.

She ran, as fast as her pregnant body would let her, and entered along with her husband into the gates of the fort. Out of the corner of her eye she saw her Uncle Benjamin parlaying with the Indians who looked sternly down upon him from horseback.

Benjamin walked slowly into the enclosure shaking his head. "There will be no peace this time," he was saying.

"We must close the gates then and defend ourselves!" his brother, Silas, exclaimed, with fierce resolution.

"Then they will kill us all. I know that I will not make it to see another day but I can delay them long enough for the women and children to escape. Some of the men too may escape. But if we hold out in the fort, they will be inside in no time and slaughter every last one of us."

"That is folly, Benjamin! We can hold out and send a signal to the Rangers to rescue us! I am for holding out!" Silas then turned to the elderly man next to him. "What say you, father?"

John the Elder, who had been listening with arms crossed and a grim look of determination on his face spoke after a few moments of heavy silence, "I am in accord with Benjamin. We will delay them as long as it takes for the women folk and children to run to the woods. There are so many, we will not be able to hold them for long."

"Then it is settled," Benjamin said, with resignation and courage chasing each other in his speech. "We will go and delay them with talk of gifts and such. Rachel," he said turning to the young mother who had gathered her two-year-old child and had been listening to the proceedings with quivering lips. "Go, save yourself and take your son to the woods as fast as you can!"

Silas was not satisfied, and before Benjamin had reached the group of waiting Indians, he jumped to the gates with his rifle. "They'll kill Ben and then me, but I'll do for one of them by G-d!"

The rifle report rang out clearly and before Rachel was able to understand what was happening, Benjamin had been cut down by the warriors and Silas was being dragged screaming from the stockades. The next moment, the Indians were inside the fort and all was lost. John lifted a clubbed gun to defend himself but was disabled by a shot to his gut and surrounded by knife wielding Comanches who finished him off piece by piece.

Rachel had not run. She feared that she along with her son would prove an impediment to the rest of the fleeing inhabitants. Her husband had seen her exit the fort and then stop, watched helplessly from the woods as she and the child were surrounded by whooping, raving braves with the light of destruction in their black eyes. Knowing that to attempt to fight was to sacrifice himself and any hopes of regaining his family, he did the only thing possible and fled deeper into the woods, his wife's screams pursuing him as he ran.

In the fort, another child had been trapped before she was able to flee. This was the nine year old Cynthia Parker, daughter of Silas. She was a beautiful child with striking blue eyes and long, brown tresses. She stopped running as soon as she realized she was trapped and stood there proudly awaiting her fate at the hands of the savages.

Suddenly, from the group of warriors jumped a young brave, tall and well-built. He shielded the captive white girl from the grasp and evil intentions of the carousing group. When they saw the determination in his eyes, even the bravest or most wild (a very thin line separates the two) among them dared not take her away from Peta Nacona, the chief's 's eldest son.

1. A Treasure Lost and Found

Don Carlos

An Antelope Jackrabbit ordinarily spies a threat and takes off in the opposite direction. This particular animal wasn't given a chance to do so. No sooner had its nose begun to twitch as it sensed someone looking in its direction than the bullet pierced its chest and sent it careening across the dry desert floor. Coming to rest on its side, it had not yet ceased convulsing when it was gripped roughly by a brown hand.

"Hey there, buddy! Yer gonna share that, ain't ya?"

The brown-handed man turned his dark visage towards the speaker. "Well now, sir. If you want it, I suppose you can shoot just as fast as I can." His lip curled into a grin and a row of bright teeth became visible. He raised his gun a bit menacingly and rested it on his thigh.

"Now, Don Carlos," the other man chattered nervously, "I didn't mean nothin' by askin'. I just was hungry, you see. We're all hungry."

"Yes, I do see. It's a shame what happened out there, isn't it? Well..." he said, turning back to the dead animal and pulling out his knife to strip the fur from it. "We've got to do the best we can with what we've got. Now, I'll be fair with you lads. I'll eat it, and when I'm done, if there's somethin' left for you, I might throw you all a bone or two."

"Me an' the fellers would be mighty glad for it. Thank you!"

"Yes, I suppose you would…" His voice trailed off as the images of the horrible incidents of a week ago came back to him.

Everything seemed to be going well. They were making good time and the weather had held up. No storms or wind or heat. Just easy sailing, as it were.

One evening they were sitting around the fire and partaking of the ample victuals provided by the sponsors of the expedition. The firelight made a cheery contrast to the cool, dark, moonless night. Then, from nowhere it seemed, out on the pitch-black plains, the outlaws rode up to the wagons which were neatly circled for the evening.

The first sign that these fellows meant trouble was the black masks on their faces. They proceeded to surround the camp, as if it had been a choreographed dance, with rifles raised.

Then one of them, much larger than the rest, ordered the others to disarm the men gathered around the fire.

The marauders received a few dirty looks from the men whose guns they took but were cooperative, mainly because of the commanding position of their enemies on horseback. Nothing makes as good a case for compliance as a Winchester Rifle pointed at one's head.

"Who's in charge o' this here caravan?" the giant spoke in a surly fashion. "We needs to have a talk, he and I."

The hand standing next to Don Carlos started to speak, pointing next to him at the trail boss when he was given a good crack on the head by a butt end of a pistol.

The man crumpled to the floor and the head desperado looked over at Don Carlos.

"Now what happened?"

"Oh, he was starting to turn yellow and was going to try to run. I just made sure he stayed here with the rest of us."

"Well, it's a good thing you did 'cuz I woulda shot 'im outta his boots if he'd tried to run! Maybe he owes you a debt o' thanks or I'm wrong."

"Maybe he does…" Don Carlos agreed in a low voice.

The man, who dwarfed his black horse, bellowed, "Well… seeing as how none o' you has the guts to speak up, we'll just have to take everything instead o' just the headman's stuff!"

This was too much for the men who all looked at their leader pleadingly. He seemed not to be ruffled by the words of the outlaw. Their eyes seemed to say, "Please just admit who you are!" but those pleas fell on deaf ears, so to speak. None of the men dared argue with Don Carlos or point him out, as he was a known killer and the fastest shot any of them had seen.

"OK then! Men, gather up all the provisions and put them up in that there wagon, take their horses, and burn the rest!"

McGovern, a young hand with a fresh face was trembling and said, "We… you just can't…We'll starve. We're as good as dead!" His last sentence had been delivered with a bit more emphasis.

The giant whirled on his mount and looked down from far above at the boy, his eyes smiling cruelly from behind the mask.

"Well now, boy, would you rather I shot you here instead?"

The youth looked up with hatred in his eyes momentarily, and then seeing the fruitlessness of further resistance, turned his eyes toward the ground. He kicked a stone with a well-worn boot and shook his head.

"I thought as much," roared the big man with a laugh. He was joined by his comrades who seemed to always look to their leader for permission to act.

With the wagons alight and the horses being led away, the behemoth on horseback turned back to face the brooding members of the caravan. He slowly lowered his mask to reveal fine, large features and a bristling nut-brown beard. It was a countenance they'd all seen in the saloon before leaving town.

"I doubts any of you will ever make it back to civilization, so I don't mind showing you who you've been bested by!"

Don Carlos seethed inside and swore revenge on the man if ever he saw him again. If not, he hoped that another would exact it on the outlaw.

Picked Men

The instructions from back East were to find a crew to dig up the silver that was to be found back in the creased hills of Oklahoma, near the headwaters of the Red River.

This wasn't just any old silver, however. It was fine Spanish silver that had been left there by wandering Conquistadors who had met their fate at the hands of the Apache. The bricks of precious metal were reported to weigh upwards of ten pounds each. Trading at $1.38 per ounce, the fine silver ingots brought to market by enterprising Indians were worth nearly $222, and there were supposedly thousands waiting to be unearthed. In the colorful language of the plains people, there were "as many as the leaves of the forest".

That news had created a bit of an exploratory rush, and Rogers' employers had purchased a large chunk of property right smack in the middle of it all. They had entrusted Ned Rogers, the former Civil War adjutant, to recruit and lead the men in the endeavor and bring back as much of the precious metal as possible.

Being honest with himself, Ned couldn't quite understand why they had chosen him. He was more comfortable behind a desk counting other people's money. He reasoned that he had been picked for the job because he was trustworthy. And he was, to a fault. He would never touch a penny that was not his own. Greed or avarice were not a trait anywhere on the horizon of his consciousness. Being a strong leader and a good judge of character were not among his many good qualities but, as events would soon prove, were an asset that would prove to be helpful.

Just now, as he approached the raucous saloon, he knew only one thing. He needed tough men. There were savage Indians, outlaws, wild beasts, and all manner of natural and manmade hazards to be dealt with. It didn't take a seasoned treasure hunter to realize this wouldn't be an easy task and he was aware he required steely-eyed men to handle the hunt.

The half doors swung easily on their hinges as Rogers stepped into the saloon. The contrast from the bright midday sun to the murky confines of the smoke-filled room caused him to squint. He was just able to make out the bar ahead and a great stag head staring down from it's mount high up on the wall. His eyes adjusted quickly and he was able to discern the usual set of bar-room inhabitants. The mustachioed bartender, the women of ill repute, the gambler, and the cowboy. All were well represented.

In the far corner was something out of the usual. Surrounding a green card table under a gilt light, a group had immediately caught the newcomer's attention. A burly, jovial giant of a man was holding court and his ten comrades laughed uproariously at the smallest of his jokes. He was slapping his leg with joy as he recounted some adventure or another.

This might be just who the representative was looking for! He might even hire them all in one fell swoop instead of hiring individually. They certainly looked like a tough lot, but something in their easy movements, and the sheer size of their leader, spoke of capability.

Rogers stood there, nearly unnoticed in the light streaming in from the front door for a moment. He gathered his courage, squared his shoulders, and then slowly approached the table in the back.

No sooner had he come within four feet of the table when a yellow skinned man jumped into his path. The man stood so close to Rogers that he was able to pick up the reek of alcohol on the other man's breath.

"Who might you be?" the saffron colored apparition asked, his eyes casting suspicious glances up and down the newcomer.

"Ned Rogers, of the Amalgamated Silver and Mining Company, Pittsburgh Pennsylvania, at your service."

The bile-shot eyes narrowed. "And what are you wantin'?"

"Merely to speak with your friend there," he replied, nodding towards the big man who had stopped laughing to glare warily at the stranger.

"What of?"

Mustering more courage than he would have given himself credit for, he spoke over the guard's shoulder. "To hire you and your men, sir! A more than fair price will be paid by my employers and there will be shares of the booty for each of you."

"What does he want then?" boomed the bass voice from the corner. The room fell suddenly silent. "Let him pass, Florio."

Ned squeezed past the sentinel with a polite smile and stood before the huge man.

He extended a trembling hand which was grasped by the hairy paw of the other, enveloping the easterner's hand completely. It was a grip that the latter felt might break every bone in his hand.

"Ned Rogers sir, Amalgamated Silver and Mining Company, Pittsburgh Pennsylvania, and we're looking for a few good men for our expedition. Is here a good place to talk?"

In response, the giant swept the felt table clear of cards, cigars, glasses, and bottles with a motion of his huge arm. A smile creased his fine features and his nut-brown beard moved like a living thing when he finally spoke.

"Jim Veroba's my name and here's as good a place as any! Have a seat, Mr. Rogers!" he bellowed.

The Abduction

Blood. Blood on his hands, on his moccasins, on his shirt. Blood covered him, yet there was hope in his heart. Charlie had completed his mission and the enemies were no longer of this earth.

Was she safe? The possibility of harm having befallen his love hung in his mind like a specter.

Reaching the seldom-traveled path, he stopped to listen as the last light of the sun turned the world shades of red, purple, and then indigo. There were no sounds, only silence and then the coo of a dove. Once and then again, the soft sound whistled from behind some rock outcropping on the cliff face. Charlie responded with a signal of his own, slightly lower in pitch. Sign and countersign confirmed, another of his tribe appeared only a few feet away, standing briefly in the fading light.

He could see Quanah, his adopted brother and son of Chief Peta Nocona, appear from behind a rock outcropping. These were tough days for the Comanche and they had to be extremely careful, especially after an action of this kind. White men were dead by the red man's hand and that carried consequences. One false move and an Indian brave may end up either food for the buzzards or languishing in a stockade in some Texas town. Both options were undesirable, with vulture food being the more honorable choice.

"You have her?" Charlie whispered.

Quanah merely nodded and held a finger to his lips, a look of rebuke evident on his brown countenance.

Charlie realized immediately that he should not have spoken. His white heritage betrayed itself occasionally, although he'd lived for nearly twelve years among the Quahadi—or antelope eaters—of the Wichita Mountains in southwest Oklahoma. A true-born warrior never would have spoken out loud, but rather would have used the simple, yet efficient sign language that the tribe employed for warpath communications.

Now, as they slunk away into the weird and wild crags that rose from the desert, Charlie allowed himself a smile, partially from relief and partially from happiness. He was focused entirely on the thought of seeing his Little Wing again.

Little Wing, the Comanche princess who had descended from a very prominent family and later joined the band headed by Peta Nocona, was his intended. They would be wed within the next few weeks. Some said that her family went back earlier than when the Buffalo had been set free. She was perhaps, and according to all who saw her, the most physically enchanting woman this side of the Wichita Mountains. In fact, her beauty may have been the reason why Charlie had needed to take lives that day.

It had happened this way: A rowdy band of treasure hunters with evil intentions had happened upon his bride-to-be when she was out gathering some berries for the camp in a canyon and had spirited her away. She had been carried back to their encampment in the mountains, where they had been hunting for an old hoard of Spanish gold. Little Wing had been locked in a prison shack with either ransom or a worse purpose in mind.

Charlie had heard screams from the creek where Little Wing had been foraging and leapt on his pony, riding as if the world were afire! The few moments he took to arrive were merely a blur in his mind and his pony was foaming when he reached the canyon. Nearly skidding off a cliff, he arrived just in time to catch a glimpse of the captors. A few pebbles dropped down the hundred or so feet to the floor of the crevice.

One of the men stopped and looked up at the sound, but Charlie had already backed his horse away. When the rogue glanced up, all he glimpsed was the outline of the cliff against a white-blue sky. He warily examined the area for a moment longer and shrugged, continuing on his way to catch up with the others.

The warrior peered over the edge of the cliff to see the miners jolting along the mountain path on their weather-beaten horses through a crevice in the rocks.

Charlie's fists balled in anger and his gut wrenched tightly at the sight of Little Wing bound and trussed in ropes, slung haphazardly over the back of a horse, and struggling with all her might to get free.

Charlie cursed the men and began the laborious task of tracking the scoundrels to their lair, his desperation tamped down and kept in check by his desire to save his love.

The miners did not notice they were being trailed, laughing at their luck in finding a "squaw princess." They spoke in drunken voices about their plans for after they'd reached their home base.

A bear of a man appeared to be their leader, a person whose immense size dwarfed his horse—as if he were riding on a pony, although his steed was full sized. He was shouting something in a slurred voice, his gigantic nut-brown beard shaking violently as he spoke. Dressed in clothing typical of the place and time, he wore brown boots with rusty spurs, dull leather chaps and a black vest over his dirty shirt, topped with a dark-brown, brimmed slouch hat that was stained in various places.

"When Rogers sees this here prize," his resonating bass voice bellowed while pointing at Little Wing, "he'll jump out of his skin!" He then laughed heartily until he nearly choked, and the others joined in the raucous laughter.

Catching his breath, the big man continued, "We're gonna be rich, mates! Rogers can say what he wants about finding the motherload, but there ain't nothin' in these mountains worth a darn! We've been here for months and been digging for the past thirty days or more without findin' hide nor hair of gold, nor a sliver of silver!"

"He's right on that point!" a slim, leather-skinned man said in a high-pitched rasp, which had been roughened by smoke and miles of trails. He bounced along on his nag and continued, "We're so backed up on pay that I'd be surprised if we see a penny now!"

"True for you, Smith!" the giant exclaimed. "And as sure as my name is James Andrews, I'll see to it we get our fair share from this squaw! Are you all with me?"

"Aye! Yessir! I'm with Big Jim!" a chorus of affirmative answers tumbled forth from the unruly gang.

"It's decided then! We'll split the pot o' this here ransom whether it be gold, trinkets, horses, buffalo, or whatever these savages are willing to trade for her and..." Big Jim proclaimed, stifling a belch, "maybe if he's real nice, we'll let Rogers in on the cut!"

"Aye! Indeed! That's it!" they all shouted.

And with that, they fell into small talk amongst themselves, commenting on their unbelievably good luck and fortune.

Little did they know that they were being trailed by one of the fiercest Comanche warriors ever to pick up the lance in battle.

Once the party of ruffians had arrived at their camp, Charlie Bird made sure to find out where they were holding his bride-to-be captive and headed back to his camp under the soaring cliff to summon the other warriors. He might have taken care of all of them himself after nightfall, but it would be much quicker with some of his tribal brothers. Their presence would also reduce the risk of Little Wing being injured or harmed during the rescue attempt.

Setting the Stage

The mining camp was surrounded by Comanche warriors silently waiting like ghosts in the hills for the signal to commence the attack. Without a sound, Charlie crept behind some tents and craned his neck to survey the layout.

A few flies buzzed about, but there was very little movement. It was the heat of the day; almost every man was in his tent sleeping off whatever he had drunk that morning. One of them had gotten up to relieve himself and then crawled back inside his tent—moments later, he was already snoring like a buzz saw. The yellowish cur that was more of a companion than a guard dog sat lazily in the shade, its dusty tongue hanging from a slack mouth.

A huge pair of boots stuck out from the flap of one of the green canvas tents, and the grunt that escaped the tent sounded like the growl of a nearby bear. A few murmurs and snorts and the boots turned as their owner tried to find a more comfortable position before finally coming to rest.

Toward the center of the encampment was a dusty, ramshackle shed that stood fringed on two sides by the stunted desert weeds. The building was dilapidated in appearance yet had a sturdy-looking wooden door. A small, square-like hole looked to be the only means of ventilation. Charlie Bird made his way toward the crooked edifice using all the tricks he had learned while in the company of the Comanche to remain silent, his movements making nary a sound.

Keeping his body low, he slunk along the side of the shed and peered through a crack in the wood. He was startled for a moment by what he saw, immediately jerking his head back from the opening. After several moments, he regained his composure and looked again.

Inside the shack was a man tied to a pole with rags. His head hung listlessly, and in the low light of the shack he appeared to have been beaten rather severely. The man was still breathing, but how long that would continue was an uncertain thing.

The Comanche had expected to find his intended, but instead had found this. Charlie guessed it was that man Rogers the miners had referred to back in the gully. He must have upset the men and gotten shackled as a result. If Rogers was right there, however, then where was Little Wing?

He took a chance and made a tick with his tongue to grab the prisoner's attention. Rogers made a movement and then opened an eye. He looked around in a surprised manner, as if he was expecting another beating at the hands of his captors.

Charlie clucked again and the man cast his glance around, looking for the source of the sound. He stopped when he noticed the eyeball looking back at him from the lower corner of his prison.

"What... What are you about?" he mumbled.

"Shhh," Charlie warned. "If you make too much noise, you'll turn this place into a hornets' nest."

"OK," the man said in response. Then, in a softer voice, he added, "Who are you?"

"I may be your savior. But where is the girl?"

"The girl? Oh, you mean that Indian squaw they captured up in the hills?"

"Yes!" Charlie Bird hissed through clenched teeth. "Where is she?"

"She's in the next room. Right over thar," Rogers said, nodding toward the far wall. "This here she's got two rooms with a wall between 'em. I dare says she's in better shape than I am though. Say boy, can you spring me from this pen? I don't think I can handle another beating like that." As the words left his lips, the man broke into soft sobs.

"OK... OK, quiet now. Get a hold of yourself. I'll tell you how we can get you out of this, but you have to follow my instructions to the letter."

The man said nothing in response, but nodded profusely. With that, Charlie proceeded to tell the trapped man how to conduct himself during the rescue attempt that would follow.

Next, he made his way along the outside wall toward the other side of the shack. When Charlie reached Little Wing's holding cell, he pried a plank loose. The slight snap made the old dog look up from his spot in the shade, but Charlie had been careful to remain upwind of the animal. Not sensing any danger, the dog lay back down in the cool dust. Charlie looked inside for his beloved Little Wing.

As Charlie's eyes adjusted to the dimly lit interior, he was able to discern a huddled form in the corner. She appeared to be sobbing, which made his chest tighten more and more with each step in her direction.

Hoping to draw her attention the way he had with Rogers, Charlie clucked with his tongue until the girl looked around, startled by the noise.

In his native Comanche language, he called out to her softly, "It's me, my little bird. Are you OK?"

The look of relief spread across her beautiful, tear-stained face as she realized her hero had arrived. She crawled out from her corner and reached her hand towards her intended.

"You are here!"

"Shhh... I am here, and I will save you... but you must be quiet." Charlie couldn't hold back a smile, despite the seriousness of the situation. "I'll get you out of here, but you must follow my instructions. Understood?"

"Yes, of course," she said, smiling back at him.

With that assurance, he explained his plan to her and gave her a signal that would mean the rescue was commencing. He smiled again and reached his hands into the building, grasping Little Wing's hand briefly before disappearing amongst the weeds that ringed the hut.

Charlie crawled away from the camp having seen what he needed to see and planned what he needed to plan. He silently called to his brother warriors in a sign language unique to his people to explain things. Sitting Bear would descend from the north to carry out his part of the plan, Quanah would come from the east to block any means of escape, Charlie would come in from the front to begin the game, and the other seven tribesmen would provide cover and keep the enemy's heads down.

Aspirations and Endings

James Veroba had always imagined that he'd been royalty in a past life. Perhaps a duke or baron. He had a majestic air about him, accompanied by a natural charisma that made people listen to his plans and act accordingly. He always delivered his bombastic proclamations with a touch of superiority, and those around him always bowed to his superior intellect and ideas.

Just now he was riding his great white horse across the green moors of the English countryside, toward the sound of battle. A great crag of granite rose to his left like some leviathan of an ancient world, and the smell of wet vegetation hung heavy in the air.

As he crested the hill overlooking the fighting below, he spied a lithe man in royal purple robes, seated on a white horse with his sword raised, and surrounded by armor-clad warriors as he fought valiantly for his life.

James roared mightily and spurred his horse down the incline to save his king.

"Richard! Hold fast! I am coming!" he yelled, before roaring out his battle cry yet again.

The knights surrounding the king wheeled about on their own horses as the gigantic warrior descended like a storm on his adversaries. One of the rogue knights turned and began barking at him. What was this?

Then the barking of his dog woke Jim from his afternoon nap. A streak of sunlight broke through his tent, marking dusty streaks in the air. He closed his eyes and rubbed them before stretching out to his full length as he prepared to see what that darn dog was carrying on about.

"Durn varmint," Big Jim Veroba muttered to himself. "It was a good dream, too. I'd best go see what the mutt wants!"

He stretched once more and sat up with a grunt. Without putting on his hat, he ducked out of his tent and straightened to his full six feet and six inches.

"Now shut up, you flea-bitten—" He stopped mid-sentence when he saw the Indian.

A handsome but clearly inebriated Native was stumbling toward the miner's camp and yelling some incoherent thing in his native tongue. Drunken Comanches were nothing new in this part of the world. Everyone knew the indigenous people had issues with the white man's fire-water, but this particular Indian had blue eyes. *How strange*, Big Jim thought.

He shook off his surprise and called to the man, "What are you about around here?"

The staggering man looked up and grinned, but then just continued rambling toward the collection of tents.

"Shut yer yap, dog!" Jim screamed at his canine companion. Then he called to his compatriots, who had already begun to wake from their drunken slumbers because of the giant's raised voice.

The men gathered at the center of their camp, scratching various itches and rubbing their eyes to see what the commotion was all about.

"Stop now, my good Indian friend, right where you are! What do you want?"

Again, no response was forthcoming from the young man— just another stupid grin. This time, however, he stopped. He then tilted his head and regarded the big man and his collection of miscreants.

"Now, you drunken sot, what do you want here? Either state your business or be on your way! Or maybe you don't speak English?"

Once more the Indian flashed his awkward smile, but he never budged from his spot; he just stood there, swaying slightly and grinning.

"OK then, Mr. Drunken Indian! Boys! Let's escort him out of our camp. Shall we?" And with that, the men began to close in on the Native while grumbling various threats.

"Let's show him how we treat scallywags like him!" said one of them.

A skinny, yellow-eyed miner with a stooping gait stepped closer than the others. He quickly reached out his hand, grasping the Native tightly by his hair. Suddenly, the smile disappeared from the young brave's face. In its place was a cold sneer.

The thin man with yellowish eyes withdrew his hand as if he had just touched a hot stove. "What is that about?" he said, turning his face halfway from the stranger but keeping one of his eyes on the man.

Before he could say more, the young brave whipped out a large, six-shot colt pistol from under his tunic. As quick as a flash, he shot the tawny-eyed man straight through the head. Blood spurted from the wound and the man gave one final groan before dropping in a heap on the dusty ground. The others jumped back and froze momentarily, the shock of the incident paralyzing them.

This did not last long, and each man was soon reaching for his own firearm. But the few seconds of delay were far too many for the miners.

The young brave gave a blood-curdling yell and began firing with his colt and another gun that he drew from the other side of his shirt.

Big Jim roared like a bear, lifting a shovel off the cold dirt as he charged the young Native fiercely. Before five paces, he was dropped by several rifle rounds. Charlie's compatriots had joined the fray, evening the odds.

Miners fell by the twos and threes as more shots poured in from the surrounding hills. The Comanches stormed down from the heights using their Winchester rifles to pick off men at will.

As the fight reached its climax, another member of Charlie's tribe snuck into the shed and released Rogers first, soon followed by Little Wing. Charlie's instructions had been to remain inside until he signaled that the prisoner could leave, but Rogers paid no heed once he was free and immediately rushed for the door. In his haste, he stumbled out into the glaring afternoon sun, barely able to see anything for miles. Unfortunately for Rogers, he wouldn't have much time to enjoy his newfound freedom. Within seconds, a rifle blast sounded, sending a single bullet to pierce his heart. The startling impact caused him to crumple over without so much as a sound.

Thankfully, Little Wing had listened to Charlie's instructions and remained in the shadows of the shed. The fight raged on as she crouched inside, praying that Charlie Bird was still safe.

Across the camp, Charlie was trapped behind a barrel, defending himself from some miners who had managed to gain cover behind the camp's well. They were firing in his direction every time he attempted to get a shot off, effectively pinning him in place.

Suddenly, the firing from behind the barrel stopped, and the two miners looked at each other. Had they hit their mark, or was this a ruse? They decided to sit tight and wait for further developments.

One of them, Monk by name, cautiously looked around the rough stones of the well toward his erstwhile adversary's position. A hand flopped down and lay limp in the dirt, the gun it once held tumbling out of its grip.

Monk then turned towards his companion. "I think we got 'im! Look for yourself!"

The other miner, Chambers, rolled around and looked for himself. The hand was still there!

"I do believe we shot the savage, Monk!"

With that, they made their way ever so cautiously toward the barrel, guns drawn and cocked. As Monk rounded the curve, the hand suddenly sprang to life and grabbed the gun it had dropped. Within a second, Monk lay dead and Chambers was looking down the barrel of Charlie's colt pistol.

He whimpered, "Please, please... I've never hurt anyone! Please, just let me go!"

Charlie thought about it, but just for a very brief moment. The shot rang out clear and crisp, and Chambers was no more of this earth.

The Silence of Victory

The sudden quiet that descended over the camp was astounding in how very loud it was. Seconds before, guns had been blazing and horses neighing amidst a general melee; and now... there was nothing.

A dog limped out from behind the tumbledown building that served as the general store and began to pick at one of the miners sprawled on the ground. Then, curling up in the way dogs sometimes do, he settled down with a whimper next to his master.

Charlie Bird slowly stood up from behind the tar barrel he had been hiding behind. After blowing on the barrel to clear the smoke, he placed his revolver back in its holster. His deerskin breeches were covered in miles of road dust with a faint trace of blood. The war paint had begun to run with sweat, and his moccasins were worn down from trudging through the mountain paths and crevasses of the area. Overall, he looked a mess.

The scene, had it not been for the recent carnage, was actually quite beautiful. It appeared as if painted by a master hand, varying colors of earth forming striations on the buttes that ringed the mining camp. With a setting sun and the rose-colored rays silhouetting the stunted Joshua trees and saguaro cacti, it was a sight that could make one thank G-d he was created. A cool breeze blew softly, stirring the tumbleweeds.

The strident call of an Indian brave echoed from the walls of the empty stores. *These* were his people, and he called out his own countersign as he ran toward the hills.

2. Adobe Walls

The First Day

Sod was an expediency invented by an industrious pioneer whose name has been lost to posterity. It was a crude, yet effective way to erect a building in the days following the Civil war when the most adventurous spirits loaded their wagons and headed west. On the Great Plains there existed no giant forests with which to obtain more sophisticated building material. All one had to do was dig up the earth and grass in block-sized chunks around the proposed building site and get to work. The resulting structure was solid enough, provided shelter from the elements, retained heat in the winter, and kept the interior relatively cool in the summer. One property the inventor had probably not counted on was sod's usefulness when defending against attack.

Just now the defenders of Adobe Walls were thankful that the earthen walls effectively stopped all of the bullets and arrows the surrounding Indians could direct at them.

Billy Dixon ducked down below the rough-hewn window to reload his rifle. The sound of missiles thudding dully against the earthen walls became intense and then slackened off as the attackers reloaded. A flaming arrow sliced through the air and struck one of the defenders in the leg. The man, Mr. Olds, screamed as he grasped his wounded limb and tumbled forward onto the dirt floor, blood curling around his clenched fingers.

Billy cursed, rose up fiercely, and fired at the first Native he saw. The Indian yelped and pitched backwards from his mount. This only served to enrage the whooping host that was circling the collection of three green buildings set in a slight depression on the surrounding prairie.

Sporadic fire had been coming from the defenders for some time but Billy's shot had the effect of creating a concerted effort on the part of the trapped buffalo hunters. As if by signal, they all leaped to the windows and slots and let loose with a barrage. Several Indian saddles were emptied and the initial attack broke off. The natives retreated in military fashion and galloped towards a ridge about a mile away that overlooked the plains.

The buffalo hunters streamed out of the building with their large caliber rifles and knelt to fire more accurately at the retreating Indians.

One large chief had his mount shot from under him and he tumbled to the ground in a cloud of dust. Upon hitting the dirt, he leaped athletically to his feet and hopped on the back of another's horse who was passing by. They galloped towards the protection of the ridge together.

When they rode up the slope toward the high ground, Quanah jumped from his brother's horse and inspected his shoulder where the bullet had passed through and exited from the bottom of his neck. It was more painful than serious.

Removing a bloody hand from the injury, he looked seriously at Isatai'i, the medicine man who had promised that no bullet would pierce any warrior's body if he fought with courage and danced the sun dance.

"You said this could not happen, but look! We have lost several warriors who did not protect themselves as they should because you made them believe they were invincible! 'No white man's bullet will touch you!' you said! Well, what of it?" the chief seethed, extending his good arm in a sweeping gesture.

"I... I..." the rotund spirit man stammered.

Quanah walked menacingly up to him, towering over the trembling fraud. He bent his face to the other man's and spoke in a barely contained fury. "Their blood is on your hands. And on mine for listening to a charlatan like you!"

Isatai'i retreated a few steps. "The buffalo men must have special bullets, blessed by their Great Spirit!" He thought for a moment. "No! It is the cursed Cheyenne. They killed a skunk earlier! Bad luck! That is why they penetrate our charms! It must be so!"

A passing Cheyenne warrior looked menacingly at the medicine man upon hearing the statement, dead, black eyes promising to punish the speaker.

"I do not believe that you still believe what you are saying! I should kill you right here for your treachery!" the chief bellowed drawing the trembling Isatai'i's attention back to him.

"No, Quanah! I will go back and speak with the spirits and find a way to win the battle!"

"You will do nothing of the kind! You will stay with us and fight like a man or be cut down by my hand!"

Charlie looked on in astonishment at the fraud's insolence in sticking to a story that he knew was a lie from the beginning. In his mind, this had been a sham from the start. There was only one G-d that he knew and he was not involved in crazy dances and medicine. Sometimes his ways were mysterious, but they were always rooted in reality.

Quanah smacked the little wizard to the ground with a tremendous swipe and watched him scurry off in the direction of his horse. He turned to his brother.

"I should have listened to you, Charlie. That man..." he said, spitting out the word 'man,' "was a liar and I was blinded by hope. You were right. I will learn my lesson and give more weight to your council in the future."

"That's all well and good brother, yet I think we should focus our energies not on deciding who was right and wrong, but on winning this fight. Those dirty buffalo hunters have killed off the animals that our tribe and the other people need to survive. They even left them to rot in the sun! If we can win, we will send a message that the white man will surely heed! You cannot take away our lifestyle just because of greedy profiteers in the big cities back East!"

"You are correct, my brother! Let us think of how we can retrieve the battle from the grip of disaster." Then, they sat down beneath the shade of the loan tree on the ridge and planned while Charlie dressed his brother's wound."

Volunteers Needed

James Hanrahan slowly opened the door to his saloon when the noise of battle had died away and surveyed the damage done in the attack. The sod had stood up to the assault surprisingly well. Not so the horses. They lay about the small settlement where they had fallen, some still breathing.

He called back to the men who were awaiting developments inside. They came single file from the entrance and set about the undesirable task of putting the horses out of their misery.

Hanrahan wandered about the buildings, cursing himself for not getting the army involved sooner. He had been at Dodge City two days ago and could have requested the nearby garrison to accompany him to Adobe Walls.

He checked the wagons that had been haphazardly parked about the place. Everyone had been inside during the fight, hadn't they? No. There was a boot protruding from the nearest of the wagons.

Peering inside, he knew what he would see before he beheld the lifeless, bloodied form of Tom Shadler. The unfortunate man was scalped and mutilated in the usual manner of the Plains

Indians' enemies. Slumped over the seat was his brother Bill, in a similarly appalling state, who had apparently been attempting to flee. With which horses, Hanrahan could only guess, as all of the equine type had been killed or run off.

"Come on you yella bellied dummies, help me bury these two!"

Some little coaxing was necessary since the danger of attack, while having been temporarily suspended, was far from over. The savages had in fact gathered on and about the ridge a mile or so off. Their plumes and war paint were still visible in the golden sunset. A sentry was posted to warn of any impending charge and the men got to work with shovel and spade.

The brothers were interred respectfully, with requisite wooden crosses stuck at an angle in the ground. Then, the defenders of Adobe Walls, Texas, gathered around a small fire to discuss how they would defend their little piece of earth.

They were all of an accord when it came to overall strategy. From the collective experience of living on the plains, they all knew that the Indians would have little patience for a siege. The plains warriors would mount another few attacks and, if properly beaten back, would retreat to the Llano Estacado and ambush travelers or assault settlements from the relative safety afforded by the High Plains. The questions of holding out long enough came up and so too did the idea of sending a lone rider to seek help.

Bat Masterson quickly volunteered. "I'll go! I can ride better'n most of the men here and I know the area!"

Some of the older among them vetoed the idea of sending the mustachioed young man on an errand that most viewed as a suicide mission.

"We need his shootin' ability more than we need his ridin' abilities!" Mr. Olds insisted.

James Hanrahan added his protest, "Yes we need young, strong fighters like Bat and Billy here to really give to the bucks as they come in! We have to send someone who's a good rider and knows the area but ain't as much in a fight."

"I'll ride," a young man said quietly from the shadows.

He stepped into the light cast by the fire, the brim of his hat pulled low over his eyes. The long, lean specimen was Henry Lease, a man perfect for the task at hand.

"I never was much in a siege like this here. I always prefers to fight from my horse. Besides, I ride a might better than Mr. Masterson." He winked at his friend as he continued, "And you all want the call for help to reach as fast as possible."

Masterson colored slightly at the insult but laughed heartily after a brief moment.

"I 'spose he's right!"

"Yessir, he is," volunteered Olds, who sat on a log nursing his wounded leg.

"Well then, it's settled! Lease, you ride at daybreak!" Hanrahan said firmly. "Now we've got to get back in the buildings and prepare for the attack that's sure to come. Billy, you get the first night watch and I'll take the second myself. The rest of you bed down so we'll all be well-rested for tomorrow's fight!"

Reevaluating Plans

Quanah looked out with uncertainty at the little cluster of greenish brown houses. The sun dipped below the horizon and a sea of stars emerged, countless strings of jewels in the black setting of a moonless Texas night.

He had to be honest with himself. Without enough guns and the failed incantation that would make his warriors "invincible" to injury from white bullets, even with superior numbers, they didn't stand much chance against the sharp-shooting buffalo men holed up in the outpost. There was also the matter of lowered morale due to the false prophecies, which he had admittedly fallen for, of the discredited medicine man.

Charlie stole up beside him and cleared his throat to let him know he was there, knowing full well some of the questions that were pulsing through his brother's mind.

"What are we to do?" he asked, after a few moments of silence.

The chief turned to his brother and shrugged. "For once, Charlie, I have no idea. We may have stirred up a hornet's nest and something worse."

"What do you mean?"

"I see the white man grows more powerful. Yes, Red Cloud in the north may have beaten back the army for a time, but they returned with vengeance. The United States forces have captured twice as much land as before and even forced the Sioux onto reservations. Their greed knows no bounds and they will stop at nothing to get what they want. This big army which we have is insufficient to even defeat perhaps thirty men and their guns. It will tell the white man that we are on the warpath. I fear they will send someone who will use tougher methods against us and exterminate the last of the Comanche."

Charlie began to protest but fell silent. He knew his brother was right and felt that their free life on the plains was near its end.

Burying the Horses

The sun rose bright in the freshness of the new morning. Groggy men opened their eyes and looked about. It seemed a dream to many of them, the events of yesterday. The lone sentry who stood with rifle at the corner of the stockade was the only indicator that they had not indeed imagined the rough fight of the preceding day.

"Get up men!" Hanrahan called to them as they began to stir. "We have much work to do!"

Mumbling, they stretched and scratched and did all manner of waking up things while keeping a wary eye on the distant ridge. The Indians had stayed put during the night, not venturing to ambush the sleeping buffalo men.

Mr. Olds looked curiously out the window and spoke the words most of them had been thinking. "Now, why do you 'spose they didn't attack us last night?"

"I was thinking the same…" Billy spoke, his voice trailing off. "Maybe it's a trap they're going to spring on us when we let our guard down."

"I dunno," returned the old pioneer. "Them rascals might be up to anything! I 'spect there'll be a fight before long!"

James Hanrahan interjected, "Look! We've no time for discussing it like some politicians back east. We must bury these horses or the smell will be unbearable in a short time. We'll make details. Each of you will pair up with another. One pair will dig and the other set will drag the caracasses over to the holes. Then we'll all shovel until they're covered."

A collective groan rose from the group of unwashed defenders, but they got to work, knowing that the saloon owner was right.

Observations and Arguments

Just over a mile away, and an hour later, Quanah, Charlie, and other prominent warriors surveyed the scene from atop the hill. They sat on horseback, ready to ride back to the camp which was enshrouded in the shadows cast by the ridge and alert the men for whatever course of action was called for.

"What do we do?" a Cheyenne with the unlikely name of Little Robe asked.

"We wait," the chief said calmly. "They must come out sooner or later to search for food."

"That is the way the white man fight! They sit around like old maids and do not do battle!" the warrior spoke in a burst of impatience. "We must attack like true warriors! We have always done so!"

Quanah assumed the air of a professor giving a class when he addressed the younger man next to him. "And do you see what good it has gotten us? They will beat us back again and again with their powerful guns until we run out of food and must leave to hunt. They will beat us at our own game and we must learn from our enemies about how to defeat them."

"I don't know," Charlie ventured. "Didn't one of their men escape last night to bring more men, even soldiers down here? Maybe we *should* retreat now."

This was discussed heatedly for a few minutes, when they all looked up to see that one of them had wandered from the group.

Little Robe was craning his neck to look out over the expanse between the Indians and the buffalo men.

"What are they doing now? Looks like they've stopped burying their horses and are looking toward us." He pointed, "Look! One has stepped forward from the others."

The rest of the Indians joined him and observed the strange movements of their adversaries.

The Shot

It was James Hanrahan's idea. Maybe a few shots at this distance would let the enemy know that they had no chance at a closer distance. All Billy Dixon, the best shot this side, or any side for that matter, of the Mississippi had to do was send a few large calibre bullets close enough to scare them. Show them that if they got any closer they'd be leaking out of a few new holes.

No one had any notion of the far-reaching effects of "the shot" as it came to be known.

Billy chose his weapon carefully from the arsenal of rifles leaned against the back wall of the saloon. He picked a Sharps "Big Fifty" over the Springfield and bolt action Colt .45. Having handled them all, he was most confident in the accuracy and shock value of sending the huge bullet the Sharps threw screaming over their heads. If he loaded it to .50-110 specification, it would go the distance, nearly a mile, and then some. True, you could load it with a bigger bullet in the .50-90 configuration but that was only good for about a hundred yards or so. No, he wanted to really spook the Indians milling about on the ridge and this setup would do it just fine.

Stepping into the sunlight, Dixon gauged the wind with his finger. It was nearly still, which meant he'd only need to adjust for drop. Perfect.

The crowd of his fellow defenders parted to let him through and then closed up again to watch the proceedings. A few men spoke in low tones but hushed as the tall, lanky figure strode to a spot he felt would serve him best. Nothing stirred as he raised the rifle to his shoulder, the white clouds dotting the clear blue vastness of the Texas sky like balls of cotton. Pressing the burled walnut stock to his shoulder, he became one with his weapon. His breathing slowed to almost nothing and the rest of the world disappeared. Only Billy and the target existed. He exhaled and held his breath. At the climactic moment of concentration, he eased the trigger back and then it was done.

The world came rushing back in the form of the cheering from his mates. They ran over and clapped him on the back.

"That was the best darn shot I ever did see!"

"You picked off a chief, feathers and all, clear across this here country!"

"Boy, if we ever get outta here, I'm buyin' you a beer in Dodge City!"

James Hanrahan was beaming from ear to ear, stepping forward to hug the young marksman with barely contained admiration.

"That was certainly a trick, young man!" the saloon owner was saying, slapping his thigh with delight. "If they don't run now, I'll be damned! Whew! That was something else, sir!"

Billy smiled back, grinning like a schoolboy. "Well, it was a lucky one," was all he could manage to say.

Someone called out, "Look at 'em run! There they go!"

And it was true. The Indians rode off the top of the hill in single file and disappeared into the surrounding plains, one chief lighter.

They all grabbed BIlly and hoisted him to their shoulders, crowding into the saloon for a well deserved drink.

"This round's on me!" Hanrahan called, as they all squeezed through the door.

Dejection

Nearly a mile away, Little Robe had breathed his last.

The sound of the rifle followed the impact of the bullet, so great was the distance. The chiefs had been looking at the defenders and attempting to decipher the meaning of the lone rifleman's queer actions. Next thing anyone knew, Little Robe had pitched backward from his mount and landed with a sickening thud on the ground, a neat, one-inch hole punched through the very middle of his chest.

Quanah leaped from his horse and cradled the young warrior's head in his arms, but he could see that it was too late. A few gasps and the Cheyenne warrior expired, his eyes staring vacantly into the great beyond.

This was too much for the Indians and they all, as if by a secret signal, mounted their horses and prepared to ride away from the cursed hilltop.

Quanah stood, raising his hand to stop them, but Charlie gently pulled his hand down.

"There's no need to stop them. It won't do any good to stay."

The chief could see the wisdom of his brother's words and he mounted his own horse dejectedly.

"Let's go and hunt, little brother. What few animals that are left will have to be enough for the Plains People this winter." Without another word, he joined the others and rode off into the setting sun.

Charlie glanced back once more at the white men—his people—who had wreaked so much havoc and would continue to do so for the foreseeable future. There was just no stopping them and their push to grab and possess anything their hearts desired.

Sighing, he turned his horse and spurred it forward to follow the others off the ridge.

The Medicine Man Gets What's Coming to Him and the Saving of Henry Lease

Firelight flickered in the Texas night, illuminating the macabre scene. Stripped to the waist, tied in cords, mouth stuffed, the medicine man writhed under the repeated blows that rained down on him from all sides. A Cheyenne brave raised his bloody club for another blow. It came down with a sickening, bone crushing sound which made Charlie wince. Having seen enough torture to last him a lifetime, he rose and walked briskly towards the nearby woods.

He could never understand the dichotomy of the Indian nature that while allowing for easy, good-natured humor and a friendly demeanor could just as quickly subject their enemies to the wickedest of treatment. He scratched his head as he puzzled over the idea and sighed.

Hunkering down next to a large tree, he stared out into the warm darkness. What was to become of the free life he so cherished? When the white man finally decided they wanted the Llano Estacado for themselves, he knew nothing would stop them. They'd come in with their iron railroads and big guns and take whatever they so desired without regard for the inhabitants of the precious land. He clenched his fist and pounded his thigh in frustration. It was maddening.

Charlie started. There was a small noise, a whimper, from the brush just beyond the clearing he was facing. Walking stealthily forward in the moonlight, he approached the spot and listened intently.

There it was again! Charlie Bird withdrew his knife and crept around the side of the bushes. He parted the branches and looked down. A pair of white, frightened eyes looked back at him.

Charlie leaped back with a gasp and prepared for whoever it was to charge out at him. When nothing happened, he made his way back slowly and pushed the bushes back again. The same eyes stared up at him, blinking.

The face that the eyes belonged to winced in pain and there was a pleading weakness in the expression. He merely whimpered and stared, seemingly unable to move.

Charlie Bird looked the man up and down, searching for a wound that left him in such a condition. It took a few moments but he saw it finally. A bullet had passed through his neck between his shoulder and where his jaw began. It seemed to have bled considerably, which explained the weakened state of the injured man.

The screams of the medicine man echoed across the forest, making the injured youth quiver even more.

"Don't let them find me," he stammered weakly.

Charlie looked back over his shoulder and shook his head. "I…"

"If they find me they will do that to me too!" he gulped, pleading.

"I will do what I can. What is your name?"

The young man couldn't believe his ears. This Indian was speaking perfect English!

"Henry," he finally returned. "Henry Lease."

"And how did this happen to you?"

"I…I was going for help during the fight at Adobe Walls. I snuck…" He swallowed back some blood and seemed too weak to continue, but he rallied. "I snuck out of there and was riding away when I heard a gun go off and felt something burn through my neck. I didn't see who shot at me and I didn't stick around to find out but rode until I must have passed out. Where's my horse?" He started to get up with a renewed energy, but Charlie pushed him back to the ground.

"You're not strong enough to go looking for your horse just yet. Also, if you get up they'll see you, and you're as good as dead if they find you. I'll see if I can find your horse but first we've got to dress your wound. Stay here." And with that, Charlie flitted off into the moonlit trees, leaving Henry to wonder at his present circumstances.

The warrior returned in short time with a crude bandage and some water, half of which he gave to the young scout to drink and with the other half, rinsed the bloody wound.

When he had finished quietly dressing the wound, Charlie spoke again. "Now Henry, we've got to get some food in you so you can have enough energy to leave."

He rose again and returned shortly with broth made of beef and steaming water and spooned it out to the stricken American, who gulped it greedily. The young man's strength seemed to return with every mouthful and he was sitting within a few minutes.

Speaking in hushed tones, Henry asked, "Who are you and how did you get to be mixed up with a bunch of Indians like this?"

Charlie smiled and answered without any trace of indignation towards the young scout. It was, after all, a good question. "I've been with them for some years. They are my people now so I never really got mixed up with them. I'm a warrior as much as the other braves."

"But you're not! You speak English bettern' I do and you have blue eyes!"

"True, but I am one all the same. My name's Charlie Bird." He extended a hand which was grasped by the other.

"Pleasure to meet you, Mr. Indian. I guess I have a lot to thank you for!"

Charlie smiled and said, "I guess you do, but don't worry about it for now. Maybe you'll repay me later. Maybe not. I just don't have the heart to turn you over to my fellow warriors, that's all."

"Well, either way I'm mighty thankful!" The young man stood to his full height, brushing off his clothes with the one arm he could use.

"I found your horse."

"You did? Where?"

As if by some unseen signal, the horse poked its head from the brush and nuzzled its nose against Henry's shoulder.

"How did you…"

Charlie Bird just smiled again.

"Well, however you did it, it's wizardry or I'm mistaken!"

Another loud scream echoed across the woods.

Charlie looked over his shoulder apprehensively. "You'd better go. My brothers will come looking for me soon and if they find you…" He didn't need to finish the sentence. "Here, take this dried beef. It should last you a few days until you get where you're headed."

Henry hopped up on his horse in the blue light of the rising moon and raised his hat in thanks.

Charlie touched his forehead in response and Henry Lease was gone.

"Who was that?" It was Quanah who had appeared over his brother's shoulder.

"Just some scout," he returned calmly. "I think we shot him when he was trying to get help at Adobe Walls. He wasn't any danger and since we're not there anymore, I saw no reason not to let him go."

"It's just as well. If they found him, they'd probably send the whole army after us."

Quanah turned and walked back towards the fire. Charlie waited a few moments longer, looking off into the night before he followed his brother.

Mackenzie Triumphant

The Caprock & Llano Estacado

Charlie and Quanah slowly approached the edge of the outcropping that protruded from the caprock, which represented the easternmost border of the high plains. It was a precipitous cliff that extended for hundreds of miles, broken by the occasional canyon that cut a spectacular gorge down hundreds of feet of rock, exposing bands of colored rock until it reached the edge of the river that roared through.

The two warriors stood together in the morning light. Quanah was at least four inches taller than Charlie and all muscle. He was the fiercest of Comanche warriors and could perform amazing feats of horsemanship that stunned friend and foe alike.

Above and to the west of the caprock were the high plains themselves—a vast grassland that seemed to stretch for miles, as far as they could see. Not a thing would stir on a hot summer day, and many a white man had died of exposure and thirst there, their bones now bleaching in the powerful sun. Worse yet were the winters when blizzards and strong winds blew fiercely across the level ground. Temperatures could drop sixty degrees in a matter of minutes, and travelers often lost their lives, frozen, only to be found by some Indian raiding party months later.

Yet, there were paths by which a man, a raiding party, or even an entire tribe could traverse this inhospitable land. A road of sorts, plentiful with water and grass for horses to graze on, wound through the tableland. Stolen horses were herded along this primitive throughway by Native Americans—Comanche, Kiowa—and traded with the Comanchero, Mexican outlaw Indian traders, for goods, trinkets, and most importantly: weapons.

The most significant feature of the plains, and what had brought the Comanche down to this inhospitable patch of earth, was the buffalo. One herd might have as many as one million lumbering members. These great beasts congregated together in populations that often stretched literally as far as the eye could see. They were relatively easy to kill and one would provide enough meat for a family for months. Their hides became cloaks and teepees, and their bones were made into tools.

The men would hunt the animals and the women would skin and clean them. A tribe could follow a herd all summer and be supplied with all their wants. When the buffalo moved, so would the people, in a nomadic sort of dance across the plains.

Such had been the situation for the Comanche for at least two hundred and fifty years, and it was a hard, free life. They had no concept of land ownership or property, and both the future and past meant very little. The present was the focus in this primitive lifestyle and aside from horses and teepees, the people cherished their freedom above all else.

That was until the white man came and began to eat away at the Comanche lands, little by little. First, it was only a few farms and trading outposts. But once the land bug caught hold, more and more people came west to take part in the limitless bounty that was the United States of the mid-nineteenth century. They pushed up to and then past the ninety-eighth meridian, which was Comanche territory.

Buffalo Men and Mackenzie

Then came the Buffalo man—the loud, raucous, unclean killer of bison for their hides. These skins could fetch as much as thirty-five dollars per piece, and because the animal was so easy to hunt—if one was killed, they all froze until the source of danger could be identified—as many as two hundred and fifty could be harvested in a single day by one man with a new Sharps fifty-caliber buffalo gun.

The indiscriminate killing of the Comanches' source of food and sustenance had led to the situation they were now in. The Native Americans, desperate to save their own livelihood, resorted to what they knew best: war. In order to stave off their own destruction, they began raiding white settlements—killing, torturing, and scalping in hopes that the hated Americans would leave. And it was working. Whites were leaving in droves, headed back east to preserve their own lives. That was until the US government stepped in and sent Ranald S. Mackenzie to head the Fourth Cavalry Regiment. He was there to quiet things down and perhaps end the "Indian menace" in Texas once and for all.

Colonel Mackenzie had lost two fingers at the battle of Jerusalem Plank Road and had been wounded on five other occasions during the recent Civil War. He was short and sharp-featured with a sour disposition, probably due to the numerous wounds he had that had never healed properly. The natives called him "Bad Hand," as much for his deformity as his skill at wiping out his opposition. No one liked him, but everyone—his enemies included—respected him. He was testy and hard on his subordinates, but they trusted him implicitly in battle. They knew he would always make the proper decision and get them out of whatever scrape they might find themselves in.

Led Astray

The Fourth Cavalry was now winding its way through the narrow defile of the Palo Duro Canyon, looking for signs of rogue Indian bands who were using the area of the Texas Panhandle as a base. The Native American scouts Mackenzie used were picking their way through the rocks and brush of the canyon floor, looking for arrowheads and tracks. They would find plenty.

Quanah and Charlie had liberally distributed various items and footprints here and there to throw off the scouts and lead them, hopefully, in the wrong direction. They watched in stillness from their perches as the Army horsemen paused at a cross in the trails and waited for the scouts to give them an indication as to which way to proceed.

The Tonkawa scout came running back, waving in the opposite direction as he said something unintelligible. The two Comanches were too far away to hear what he was saying, but the meaning of his gestures were clear. The band they were searching for had headed south—the exact opposite direction of the group they were chasing.

Mackenzie listened to the report without moving and then remained silent for a time. He raised his head and looked suspiciously about as if suspecting it was all a ruse. He had, after all, battled some pretty clever types during the war between the states, and had out-foxed a good number of them. His light eyebrows bunched together high on his forehead over glinting gray eyes as he gave the signal to proceed south.

The entire troop of two hundred and fifty soldiers turned left and trotted off, following their leader as he picked his way through the rough terrain.

The two Comanches looked up at each other and without a word exchanged knew exactly what the other was thinking. The Federals would be back as soon as they discovered they had been tricked, and that wouldn't be very long off. Bad Hand was no slouch.

It was time to move the camp.

Urgent Developments

Charlie and Quanah arrived back at the Comanche camp and informed everyone that it was time to move, yet again. The Federal soldiers were close now, and when they caught up, they would, in all likelihood, destroy the village—warriors, women, and children alike. The scent of buffalo blood and hide was strong in the smoke that drifted up from the fire.

"In there! She's ready!" the woman screeched in the Comanche dialect. "We cannot move her!"

"We must move everyone," Quanah replied, in a kindly voice that was calm and composed despite the desperate situation. "Let us see what can be done." And with that, he strode over to the tent in question, through the general melee of packing and rushing, while the old lady bounced along behind him still keening and wringing her hands.

Pushing aside the flap, Quanah looked in to see a young woman in the last stages of labor, her screams filling the tense air of the teepee. An elderly midwife sat next to her and mopped her brow while offering words of encouragement. The husband, one of Quanah's young warriors, was pacing along the other side of the room. Upon seeing his chief, he stopped pacing and rushed forward with a look of deep anxiety on his face.

"Quanah! We cannot leave yet! We cannot!"

"Worry not, brother. We will not leave you, but we must move. You must trust me!"

Stepping outside the dwelling, Quanah glanced around quickly. He spotted the man he was looking for and then motioned Charlie to him.

"Charlie Bird, I have a special mission for you!"

The smile spread across Charlie's handsome face even as he knew it would be a dangerous endeavor.

The chief spoke as he placed his arm around his friend's shoulder and led him to the horses. "Here is what I want you to do."

After receiving full instructions, Charlie approached his mount to ready it. He was headed to meet with the warriors he would be leading into battle. He needed to inform them of the plans that were to be followed carefully, because it was imperative that things went in their favor. After all, this was their last chance to save their people.

The supreme mounts the Comanche rode were horses of unusual ability and temperament. They were lithe, strong animals and were extremely sensitive to their riders' whims. Beautiful and sleek in their mottled coats, they grazed in the dusty field they had been corralled into about two hundred yards from the main encampment.

Horses have a peculiar ability to divine their masters' emotions even when they may not be apparent to the casual observer. Charlie's—Silverback was her name—could sense the tension in his demeanor now, despite his calm outer appearance. She shuffled and pranced in reflection of his nervousness, and Charlie patted her neck to calm her down.

"Good girl. Easy now," he whispered in English. He had always found that his native tongue worked better on the equestrian set, even though he was fluent in the Comanche dialect, as well as Spanish and a few other Native American languages.

Having calmed his mare, he gently tugged her reins until she followed him back to where his warriors were waiting.

"OK friends," he began, as he stooped to the ground and sketched the plan in the dust with a piece of stick. "Here is where we attack."

Feinting and Fighting

Lieutenant Dan Robins splashed the water from the bubbling, turbid creek onto his face with cupped hands. It sure was hot out here in these plains. No man's land would be a better description. The cliffs towered above the resting spot, which Colonel Mackenzie had chosen as a place to halt. The sun shone strong and fierce above the precipice. During the day a man might burn his hands on the scalding rocks, but by that very night he would freeze in want of cover. The high plains were a strange place.

The buzz of flies was the only thing he could hear, other than a few grunts of soft conversation from the men. This was not how Robins had imagined frontier soldiering. He had envisioned riding roughshod over hills and crashing through streams in pursuit of savages—resplendent in their feathered headdresses, war-whooping and thrusting with their feathered spears. The final shot from his rifle would make him a hero as the Indian was blasted from his horse. The captain of his regiment would congratulate him, and he'd be given a bright, shiny medal and a promotion as his comrades stood in awe.

Instead, he'd been tramping through the barren wilderness in pursuit of an enemy who would not show himself, if he did indeed exist. The only evidence he'd seen of them was a few footprints and some scattered buffalo bones, and that was only after having been in this forsaken country for weeks. Most of all, he needed a bath. He'd never been this dirty in his twenty years and he didn't like it one bit. No adventure; just dust and dirt and boredom. All of that was about to change.

As he squinted once more at the cliff tops, Dan thought he noticed some movement there. He shaded his eyes and peered more closely at the spot in question. It was a small protuberance of rock that a shadow seemed to have passed over. He didn't hear the twang of the bow, yet he was quite aware of the arrow shaft that dug itself into the ground a few inches from his left leg. Seconds later, another arrow hissed through the air and split his hat in twain, barely missing his head and knocking him off his feet.

The scream he let out as he fell alerted his fellow soldiers, who began yelling, cursing, and generally scrambling for their weapons in a melee that only complete and utter surprise could cause. More arrows rained down on the hapless soldiers. Some found their marks, causing the wounded to cry out in pain. Horses neighed, and blue-coated soldiers tripped over their packs in the hot sun, falling in a lump amongst the brambles that were strewn across the canyon bottom.

Mackenzie came riding up on his charger, shouting orders, waving his troops forward with his three-fingered appendage, and firing at the cliff tops with a pistol in his good hand, reins in teeth. The acrid smell of gun smoke hung in the air when, as suddenly as it had begun, all became quiet.

The arrows ceased as if a spigot had been turned off. The war-whoops ceased and the United States soldiers cautiously raised their heads, checking themselves over and then scanning for their comrades. Next, as if by mutual accord, they all raised their rifles and pointed them at the outlines of rocks high above. If any Indian showed as much as a feather above the crest, he'd be shot down by a dozen bullets.

The sound of hoofs from twenty horses echoing off the walls was the first indication of an attack from the rear. The strident cries of the Comanche party as they descended on their quarry with flashing spears served to increase the original shock of the assault.

About twenty warriors came blasting from behind a stone wall and sliced through the ranks of the United States soldiers like thin paper.

A private fell to the ground with a gash from a short battle axe. He screamed as he fell, but was caught mid-descent by his assailant on horseback and, incredibly, lifted across the pommel of the saddle. He still struggled as he became a human shield, the bullets ripping into his body from his own friends.

The Indian rode upon the next soldier and tossed his grisly armor aside. Pulling a rifle from behind his back he cocked and fired in one smooth motion, knocking another soldier out of commission.

The regiment's sergeant charged forth with a yell and six guns blazing, emptying Comanche saddles in a barrage of bullets. Seeing his warriors falling, the leader of the assaulting Natives spun his beautiful horse in whirl of mane and tail and bore down on the officer who was shooting down his adversaries with a practiced hand. Keeping low in the saddle, he was able to dodge the shots fired his way until he reared his horse skyward, coming down with a bone-crushing thud and thus ending the threat.

Now, Mackenzie broke into the melee. His sword flashed as he waded into the group of Native horsemen. A few well-placed strikes were enough to break up the wall of whooping Indians as they retreated from the whir of sharp metal. At a signal from their leader, they then turned and leapt with incredible skill over the river, dashing away up the canyon and disappearing behind an outcropping.

Only the Indian captain remained behind, facing Mackenzie from a distance of about ten paces. The federal soldiers were beginning to gather about their leader again, after having been dispersed by the initial attack. They wiped their brows and glared angrily at the lone Comanche, who was seated atop his horse as if he hadn't a care in the world.

Mackenzie's brown eyes and sandy eyebrows met the blue eyes of the Indian chief in a steady gaze. The Native then smiled and charged him with a blood-curdling scream, pulling his tomahawk free.

The practiced soldier readied himself for the attack, bringing his sword to bear. With lightning reflexes, the Comanche dodged left and blew past his antagonist, coming so close that Mackenzie could feel the breeze of his passage. The shocked soldier blinked and turned to see Charlie Bird jump over the creek and disappear in a cloud of dust.

As Mackenzie regained his composure, he and his soldiers stared after his adversary. What they failed to see was the distant column of dust signifying the retreating Comanche camp they had been seeking. It was snaking its way across the plains in the opposite direction, complete with a new, hour-old member of the tribe, who was safely ensconced in a soft buffalo robe.

The sun had begun to set on the old Comanche camp, and the scent of cured hides and cooked meat still hung heavily in the air.

With a curse, Mackenzie threw down the discarded hide of a buffalo. That hide and the remnants of a few fires were all that remained of the Indian encampment, and the frustration was evident on his light features. Months of chasing a veritable ghost had ended with this: a few worthless arrowheads, lingering smoke, and scattered bones. It was enough to make a soldier scream!

In fact, that's just what he did.

"I… I… these Indians! These savages! They will pay for making a fool of me! They will come to the registration like lambs or they will die on these plains!" he cried, while squeezing the remaining fingers of his bad hand until the skin turned white under his black leather glove.

He tossed the skin he had been holding to the ground and stalked past an open-mouthed Lieutenant Robins. Reaching the edge of the camp, the Colonel slumped down on the parched earth and stared skyward for a few moments before regaining his composure and joining his waiting troops.

His second in command, Captain Gregoris H. Landser, spoke first after some silence. "Well Colonel, where do you suppose they've run off to? It's like they up and disappeared!"

Mackenzie had never really been impressed with his subordinate, but this time he made no effort to hide it.

"You fool! If I knew that, do you really think we'd be standing here like some old maids instead of riding them down?" he said, seething.

"Well sir, it seems that we'd be better off finding a clue so's we can go git 'em!"

Rolling his eyes, Colonel Mackenzie began to respond testily and then thought better of it. Instead, he said, "Let's begin searching for some signs as to where they went. They have women and children with them, so they must have left clues. They can't have gotten far. Fan out and bring me anything you find that you think is worthy of our consideration!"

"Yes sir!" his men said, barking in unison as they began canvassing the camp.

Mackenzie stood in the center with his arms crossed, staring intently at the feathery clouds as they turned from white to pink to a deep red in the fading light.

The world was such a beautiful place and these savages were ruining it with their raids and stubborn fight against the inevitable encroachment of the white man. Yet, a man had to do what a man had to do, and so... so, here he was to make it right.

"Sir!" he heard one of his soldiers exclaim, breaking his reverie. "Sir, I think you'll want to see this!"

Bending down to examine the nearly indistinguishable marks that his underling was pointing to, Mackenzie let out a discernible grunt. The years of rough life and his old war wounds had certainly taken their toll on his body.

"Well..." He winced. "What do you make of it, Robins?"

"It's a map, sir," came the reply. "It was all a distraction, that fight down yonder. You see the line there? That was where we were camped. Over here is where we are now and that," he said, pointing at a scratch in the earth about five inches from the other marks, "is the trail the rest of the camp took while we fought them in the canyon."

Mackenzie absorbed all this as he rose to his feet with another muffled exclamation of pain. *These Indians are more astute than I first imagined,* he thought. Then he spoke his feelings. "We must change our tactics, I think. For now, let us clean up this mess and make camp here. I'll have more orders once I've had more time to think."

He walked to the dusty edge of the Comanche camp and glanced down again at his black, gloved hand. He squeezed it to restore circulation. It had an annoying way of getting cold even under the leather cover after that terrible day ten years ago. Had it been that long? If he squeezed his eyes tight against the glare, he could just see the events that left him with a mangled hand and something worse in his heart.

June 22 1864

Smoke poured out of the crater left by the Confederate shell. None of the company had survived. They had been detailed to clear abatis from the road so that the regiment could proceed unimpeded towards the Rebels in their front. Some artillery had gotten them in range and lobbed a few shells towards the blue-coated soldiers. The first few passed harmlessly overhead and the sweating Union troops kept at their task. The next projectile found its mark.

Heat and a certain hot stillness fell over the scene as the Confederate battery searched elsewhere for targets. Shortly, a ragged hand appeared above the rim of the crater. Three fingers clenched in a fist and disappeared below the surface. Some minutes later the hand appeared again followed by the rest of the arm and then followed the shoulders, head and rest of the body. Once he had dragged himself from the hole, Second Lieutenant Mackenzie lay on the parched dirt road, breathing heavily. His chest heaved with the effort of each breath but otherwise he was still. He blew the dust from his mouth upward and turned his head to regard the rift in the earth out of which he had crawled moments before. When the ringing in his head had abated somewhat, he rolled onto his belly and lifted himself upon his elbows.

His men were all gone. So too were two of his fingers. Somewhere in the debris that lay at the bottom of the crater, his pinky and ring finger mingled with the bodies of the boys formerly under his command.

Sweat poured into his eyes and he wiped it away with his good hand. He was in no condition to walk just yet, but he couldn't stay where he was. That battery might open up again or a sniper might use him for target practice. The pain and anguish of losing his command, the fact that he'd never hear those men singing beside the campfire, these were thoughts he'd just have to suppress right now. Such young, fresh faces, that would never see their best girl, their mother, their brothers and sisters again.

Peering through the dust, about a hundred yards distant, he could see a knot of grey soldiers laughing at the havoc wrought by the lucky shot. People could be so cruel. Hell, this war was a manifestation of man's indifference to the pain and suffering of others. Mackenzie swore right then and there that he would no longer take into account his opponent's humanity. They had no concern for his, so why should he care?

Just now though. Safety was the sole concern. He would do no good for their memories if he joined them in the next world, so he stayed motionless until the soldiers turned their attention elsewhere. Then, he began to inch forward painfully back to the Union lines.

Mackenzie would leave more than a few digits on the field that day. Also left behind were any remaining warm feelings for mankind. The cold hearted hatred for his enemies would be with him to his last day.

Charlie Bird had finally caught up to the traveling Comanches. Feeling proud as a peacock, he sought out Quanah to tell him just how successful he had been in allowing their people to escape.

Toward the head of the column, he spied his adopted brother riding tall on his great horse.

Spurring his horse to join Quanah, Charlie exclaimed, "Ho there, brother! We've succeeded in shaking them off!"

The older and more experienced chieftain turned toward his younger lieutenant and frowned. "Charlie, if it was as easy as that, we'd be leading our old life, hunting the buffalo in peace. These white men—your people," he said, "are not so easily turned away from their wants. Mackenzie will not give up with the bloody nose you just gave him. He'll be after us soon enough."

The young warrior's countenance fell perceptibly and he remained quiet.

Quanah, upon seeing his brother's face and the disappointment on clear display, chided him wholeheartedly, "Listen, young warrior! You've done very well and likely saved our people here today! You should be proud!" Upon seeing Charlie's smile return, he continued, "I bet you scared those blue devils so bad that their undergarments smell worse than a buffalo pile!"

"Yes! You should have seen them run! Mackenzie himself was frightened! I saw it in his eyes as I charged him!"

"There you go!" Quanah laughed, tousling his brother's hair. "Now get going to the front and make sure we stay ahead of any trouble!"

With a few deft movements of his legs, Charlie spurred his horse forward toward the front of the advancing Comanche host.

Unpleasant Truths

In a small notch of rock burned a flickering campfire, hidden from the sight of any casual observer. The smell of roasted meat hung in the air, augmented by the desert smells of brush and sandy earth. A cool, strong breeze blew in, contrasting greatly with the warmth that was emanating from the fire.

"Brother," the younger man said, addressing the Chieftain of the Comanche. "What is our next move? You and I both know that there are only so many times we will be able to escape as we did today."

The firelight beat on his high cheekbones as he turned to speak with his brother. "I know, Charlie, I know. I have no clear answer, but I trust the Great Spirit will guide us as it has in the past. What are our options? Should we become like some of our people and submit to the white man's ways? You see what happens! We die like so many squirrels from disease or their firewater. If we take that path, we will be gone in another few generations!"

"But can't we make a treaty? Come to an agreement?"

"No. I have personally seen what happens when we make a pact with them. It is empty promises and nothing more! Think of the treaty at the Medicine Lodge! Our people were herded like animals onto some reservation and none—not one—of the promises were kept!"

"True, but maybe our leaders didn't really want to compromise then, either! Perhaps there is still hope for that route!"

"Charlie, sometimes you think like a naive white man. I mean you no offense by my comment, but you have to remember that the land is what the American wants and they'll do and say whatever they can to have it. One second they are all smiles, and the next, they take your teepee! No. Negotiating and treaties are not the answer!"

"Then what, brother?" Charlie asked, slamming his hand on his thigh. He was growing frustrated.

"I wish I knew!" With that, Quanah fell silent, looking off into the darkening sky thinking back on his dealings with the white man.

What Happened at The Medicine Lodge

October 21st 1867

Charlie Bird sat atop his horse and looked on in awe at the size of the gathering. He had never seen so many warriors in one place.

The lodge itself was set back in a field that was surrounded by a thick forest of cottonwood trees.

In that building the Comanche, Kiowa, Kiowa-Apache, Southern Cheyenne and Arapaho would try to make peace with the white man.

Over the past several years, the buffalo hunters had decimated the Plains Indians' source of sustenance. The vast herds of bison were nearly wiped out and millions of the animals were left to rot in the sun while the people of the grasslands starved.

With the situation being intolerable, the Indians as a collective whole had declared war on the Americans in that part of the country. They had descended on white settlements with a savage fury and spared no one their own unique brand of depredation.

They had killed, scalped, raped and set ablaze. Nothing was spared when they attacked a village.

Back east the newspapers had called for blood, and the government, over 1500 miles away, had set up a commission to examine the facts on the ground.

That commission had determined that the best way to attain peace was to compromise. Give the Indians a protected place to live and an allowance of sorts and they would come around. They'd stop their pillaging and just ride off into the sunset of history.

That remained to be seen, however.

In the meantime, over 7,000 Plains Indian warriors had gathered together and was more fighting men than Charlie had ever seen gathered in one spot!

He gazed out over the throng and tried to identify the more eminent chiefs.

Over there was the famous Comanche elder, Ten Bears, his gait a stooping shuffle, followed by his younger advisors, straining to hear his wise council.

To his right, the great Kiowa chief and medicine man, Maman-ti or "Sky Walker", nearly seven feet tall, strode like some gigantic insect over to another council of chiefs meeting in a cluster. He towered over his fellows as they craned their necks to speak with the new visitor.

Satanta, another Kiowa chief, who would in the very near future, lead an attempt on the life of General Sherman on the porch of a Fort Sill house, gesticulated wildly to a group of feathered warriors who seemed to hang on every word. Every movement of his spoke of a power within. Woe to the enemy who crossed lances with this Satanta.

These celebrity warrior sightings fascinated Charlie, but he was looking for someone else.

Scanning the crowd, he finally spied the muscular brave seated athletically on a striking painted horse. One giant eagle feather protruded from his headband, other than that the shirtless man was unadorned by any indication of his standing as the fiercest and most capable warrior of his tribe.

Charlie kicked his horse into a trot and headed over to him calling, "Quanah!".

The big man turned at the sound of his name. A grin spread across his handsome features as he recognized the lithe figure on horseback making its way across the field.

Quanah called back, "Charlie, I did not expect to see you here!"

Reigning up in front of his brother, the younger man returned the smile.

"When I heard you were here I came right away! I've never seen anything like this! So many warriors!"

"Yes it is quite a display of power..."

The smile faded from his face as the words faded.

Charlie quickly grasped that a dark cloud seemed to have descended on his older brothers countenance.

"What is it that troubles you, Quanah?" Charlie asked

"This...," he replied, with a sweeping gesture, " is all a lie! A show so that the white man can say he acted with compassion! They mean none of it!"

"What do you mean? All the chiefs are here! All the warriors! The Americans will see this power and know nothing can stop us from keeping our way of life."

"No Charlie, this display means nothing to them. It is a mere drop in a lake! You may have heard of the great war these people fought with each other? Brother against brother?"

"Yes, I have. I met some soldiers here that say they fought in that war."

"Did they tell you anything about it?"

"Only that it was terrible and they still think of it when they sleep."

"So that is through the eyes of a soldier in the fight, but he did not see the might of the country. They had more soldiers than the leaves of all the trees of the forest! They say over two million men! There are great trains and guns as big as trees! They speak to a commander in an instant through a wire at many, many day's ride apart. I have seen all this with my own eyes! Nothing will stop them from taking our land and forcing us to the reservation!"

"Yes, but they have no horseman like ours! Red Cloud succeeded against them. Why can we not do so too?" Charlie exclaimed, with the pressure of the moment seeping into his speech, causing his voice to rise.

"It is nothing, Charlie! Nothing! Red Cloud may have won a war but he and his people will eventually lose. They—these Americans—are far too strong and they want everything! The settler will make his way, has already made its way, across the country and there will be many, many more to come!"

As they were speaking, a great movement of men began towards the bier under which the treaty was to be signed.

Ten Bears stood before the mass of soldiers, politicians, and warriors, and waited for silence. As the attendees sat in rapt attention, he delivered with the following speech in a voice more robust than his years would dictate:

"My heart is filled with joy when I see you here, as the brooks fill with water when the snow melts in the spring. And I feel glad, as the ponies do when the fresh grass starts in the beginning of the year. I heard of your coming when I was many sleeps away, and I made but a few camps when I met you. I know that you had come to do good to me and my people. I looked for benefits which would last forever, and so my face shines with joy as I look upon you. My people have never first drawn a bow or fired a gun against the whites. There has been trouble on the line between us, and my young men have danced the war dance. But it was not begun by us. It was you to send the first soldier and we who sent out the second. Two years ago I came upon this road, following the buffalo, that my wives and children might have their cheeks plump and their bodies warm. But the soldiers fired on us, and since that time there has been a noise like that of a thunderstorm and we have not known which way to go. So it was upon the Canadian. Nor have we been made to cry alone. The blue-dressed soldiers and the Utes came from out of the night when it was dark and still, and for campfires they lit our lodges. Instead of hunting game they killed my braves, and the warriors of the tribe cut short their hair for the dead. So it was in Texas. They made sorrow come in our camps, and we went out like the buffalo bulls when the cows are attacked. When we found them, we killed them, and their scalps hang in our lodges. The Comanches are not weak and blind, like the pups of a dog when seven sleeps old. They are strong and farsighted, like grown horses. We took their road and we went on it. The white women cried and our women laughed.

But there are things which you have said which I do not like. They were not sweet like sugar, but bitter like gourds. You said that you wanted to put us upon reservation, to build our houses and make us medicine lodges. I do not want them. I was born on the prairie where the wind blew free and there was nothing to break the light of the sun. I was born where there were no inclosures [sic] and where everything drew a free breath. I want to die there and not within walls. I know every stream and every wood between the Rio Grande and the Arkansas. I have hunted and lived over the country. I lived like my fathers before me, and like them, I lived happily.

When I was at Washington the Great Father told me that all the Comanche land was ours and that no one should hinder us in living upon it. So, why do you ask us to leave the rivers and the sun and the wind and live in houses? Do not ask us to give up the buffalo for the sheep. The young men have heard talk of this, and it has made them sad and angry. Do not speak of it more. I love to carry out the talk I got from the Great Father. When I get goods and presents I and my people feel glad, since it shows that he holds us in his eye.

If the Texans had kept out of my country there might have been peace. But that which you now say we must live on is too small. The Texans have taken away the places where the grass grew the thickest and the timber was the best. Had we kept that we might have done the things you ask. But it is too late. The white man has the country which we loved, and we only wish to wander on the prairie until we die. Any good thing you say to me shall not be forgotten. I shall carry it as near to my heart as my children, and it shall be as often on my tongue as the name of the Great Father. I want no blood upon my land to stain the grass. I want it all clear and pure and I wish it so that all who go through among my people may find peace when they come in and leave it when they go out."

When the great chief finished speaking, the gathered were silent as if a great hand had been clapped over their collective mouths. The weight of it all hung there for all to absorb. Men rested their chins on the hands and thought. Others looked off into the veil hiding the future, attempting to see what the new world would mean to them and their families, loved ones, tribes, governments...

The silence was broken by a tall young warrior seated in the back.

He stood to his full height and exclaimed in the Comanche dialect "I will not sign! I will not let you white men take our freedom or the Comanche way of life!"

"Quanah, please listen to the chiefs! They have decided!" a warrior seated next to him begged.

Looking about him, arms held wide, fire of the warrior in his eyes, he coldly declared, "You are all women and children! If you will not fight you will crawl to the reservation and whimper there!" and with that he stormed from the meeting, mounted his horse and rode off.

A shocked Charlie looked about apologetically before mounting his own pony and followed his brother into the woods.

The crowd sat in stunned silence for some minutes without moving.

The unspoken thought by all was that this outburst would be the undoing of the delicate peace achieved.

A blue clad major looked on with knotted brow and felt for his missing fingers beneath the black glove.

Little Wing and Charlie

Charlie stood silently contemplating the changes that were sweeping across the broad, high plains when he heard a twig snap somewhere behind him. He continued to stand still, but all his attention was drawn toward the sound. It was human in origin—of that he was sure, since no animal made sounds like that. Every one of his senses on alert, his hand slowly reached for his knife.

He then sighed with relief and recognition when his intended, Little Wing, stepped out from behind some trees. He opened his arms to gather in his soon-to-be wife.

She approached him slowly, noting the stress in his expression.

"What is the matter, Charlie? You look like you have much weight on your shoulders."

"It is nothing. Nothing at all," he said while attempting to look cheerful for her sake.

"You are not telling the truth," she intoned softly. "Something is troubling you deeply."

"Ah!" he exclaimed, turning so she would not witness the tear fall from his eye.

She quickly hurried to face him again. "You can tell me! Tell me anything!"

"Well… It's like this. Our life—the buffalo hunts, the freedom—is all coming to an end!"

"How? I don't understand!" The shock was apparent on her beautiful features.

"They—the army, the white man—will force us from our land and onto one of those terrible reservations!"

"Can't we run? Can't we escape? This is such a large country! Surely they will leave us alone if we are far enough away?"

"No, no. I know the American. I am, or was, one of them. They will not let us rest until they have *all* of our land!"

"That can't be! That can't be!" she said fervently and began to sob, covering her face with her hands.

Charlie drew her in with an embrace. There were so many things he couldn't tell her and it was tearing him up inside. One of those things, and perhaps the most distressing, was that he couldn't love her. She was not of his tribe and never would be. Much as he had acclimated himself to the ways of the Comanche, he would always be a Jew.

A Dastardly Plan

The colonel sat on a camp chair in the clear, early morning air, distractedly sifting soil with his good hand. It was an excellent occupation for his senses as he tried to see the outcome of his latest campaign to reign in the red man.

"Corporal Dan!" he called out to his newly promoted aide de camp.

"Yessir!" the young man barked as he came to attention in front of Mackenzie.

"Corporal, I want you to do something for me. Can you do it?"

"Anything, sir!"

"Anything?" Mackenzie asked with a gleam in his eye. "You're sure?"

"Yessir! I am here to do my duty!" He stated this quite emphatically, although there was a gnawing bit in the back of his head somewhere that screamed for recognition. It was telling him now to remain on guard, for this Mackenzie was ruthless and would do anything to catch his quarry.

"Well then, here is what you shall do." Mackenzie stood as he talked and began pacing the ground in front of his tent. "You will, of course, be in charge. I want you to take a few hardy fellows from our brigade, and get some native clothes for the lot of you. Paint yourselves up like the savages. Am I clear so far?"

Before giving the younger soldier a chance to answer, the colonel continued, "Then you will get some of the finer horses on these plains. I don't care if you have to steal them. Get a few of the Indian implements of war—spears, arrows, and so forth. You will become an Indian raiding party. As such, and in disguise, you will find the Comanche camp. I'm sure you will find it easier as a small group. I'll give you one of our Kiowa scouts to help you. In the darkness, you will approach the camp and steal one of their maidens. Her name is Little Wing. She will be easy to find. She is their most beautiful young woman. When she goes to gather water, you will seize her and bring her here."

Dan was starting to realize where this whole plan was going. He had seen firsthand the destruction the Indians had wrought on that mining camp back in the mountains. They had risked all to save one of their maidens. Luckily for them, it had only been against a bunch of drunk treasure hunters. They would not fare so well against an entire army brigade that was entrenched and expecting them.

"If you kill a few of their people in the process, all the better," continued Mackenzie. "You will stir them up like a hornets' nest! They will come to us, and we will settle this at our own doorstep instead of chasing them across this G-d-forsaken wilderness!"

"Yes sir, I will not have much trouble, I suspect. I will choose our best men for the job!"

"But there's one more thing, Lieutenant!"

Dan's mouth dropped at the battlefield promotion just bestowed. Now things were going places!

Mackenzie continued with an evil smile, knowing full well from his companion's reaction that he had someone who would do whatever he asked. "You'll mark the way to the camp on your way back with the hostage. I'll split the men up; half of our men should be enough to hold them back. With the other half, you will travel to the camp and slaughter whoever is left behind. With their warriors gone saving the young girl, they will not be able to defend themselves!" Dan smiled an evil smile as he warmed to the plan. "I see you are in line with me then. Remember, the only good Indian is a dead Indian!"

Dan laughed in a wicked way and smiled, revealing a row of crooked yellow teeth. Mackenzie then chuckled darkly and slapped him on the back as they set out to carry their plan forward.

Nightmares

Little Wing awoke with a start, soaked with sweat and trembling. It was another of those dreams. She was perched atop a rocky outcropping with an abyss below her. Suddenly, rough hands grasped her and dragged her toward waiting horses. These were not typical horses. They were spectral, with fire in their eyes and smoke emanating from their muzzles. Atop the largest steed sat a monster of a man. So demonic was he that he beggared description. More of a skull than anything else, his head was ringed with flames, and sword-like fangs dripped blood into his ragged slash of a mouth. He stretched out his hand to her and she willingly reached out to him. As his hand closed on hers, her own crumbled to dust.

It was the same every time. She was unable to sleep after that, and the dream would haunt her throughout the entire day.

There was something different this time, however. Little Wing wasn't quite sure what it was, yet it horrified her. There it was. That something that had awoken her. A soft, almost sighing voice pronouncing her name. It was coming from close by. Unable to resist, she felt a cold shiver, wrapped herself in a buffalo blanket, and moved toward the teepee's entrance to look outside.

It was a moonless, cold night. It must have been midnight as there was no movement in sight, aside from the shuffling of horses in their pen. The rest of her encampment was dead silent.

Suddenly, from behind the row of tents, a twig snapped. Then there was another noise, like the quiet tread of several feet moving on tiptoe.

The Indian princess froze, not knowing whether to retreat into her domicile or not, since there were several children and a few elderly women who all lay fast asleep. She could hear them breathing as they slumbered and knew that an intruder would slaughter each and every innocent person. Taking that into consideration, she decided her best course of action would be to raise the alarm. The warriors who stood guard, wherever they may be, would come running to assist.

Just as Little Wing prepared to call out, a rough hand clamped tightly over her mouth. She struggled against the pressure, but the owner of the hand was far too strong. He pulled her back toward the darkness with an iron grip.

"Shush now, darling," came a soft voice in her native dialect. The speech was so low it was nearly indiscernible. His breath was heavy, full of whiskey and decay, and so fetid that it almost made her vomit.

"If you scream out, I will kill everyone in the camp. I have it surrounded," the attacker continued. "D'you understand me?"

Seeing no choice but to comply, her shoulders sagged and she nodded her head in acquiescence.

"Good then. You will be compliant or I will have to be as good as my threat. Now walk with me." And with this, he led her forward for several minutes into the wilderness. Shortly after, they approached a few waiting horses mounted by black figures. They appeared as dark shapes, even against the blackness of the night.

The tallest of the men stretched his hand forth toward the lady, causing Little Wing to faint from fear as her nightmare was realized.

The marauders then picked her limp form up off the hard ground and tossed her like a sack of grain onto the back of the taller man's horse. One by one, they made their way back toward the army camp.

Corporal Dan smiled inwardly and congratulated himself on a job well done.

Little Wing, Again!

As the sun rose over the Comanche camp, Little Wing's absence was soon noted and the place grew abuzz with excitement. Where could she be? Had she wandered off or been spirited away? The question hung heavy in the dense air.

At first, no one spoke. A young child called from behind one of the tents. As the tribe began to crowd around the spot the girl was pointing at, gasps began to sound. The chatter rose and hovered in the air, high above the gathering.

Quanah pushed forward, always careful not to hurt anyone, followed closely by Charlie Bird,. As he approached the spot in question he could see the youth with her finger still outstretched.

She was pointing at the parched ground behind one of the teepees. People did not normally tread there much, but perhaps it had been a child at play. Upon closer inspection, however, they found that to not be the case.

It was clear that a struggle had ensued. Next to the small footprints there stood a much larger boot-print, stark against the pale earth. It appeared to be of the standard-issued army type. Most of the warriors had noticed the strange prints these boots had made on a trading parley with the army some time ago. One sole looked to have been cracked along the bottom.

If one looked carefully, it was fairly easy to determine what had occurred. A collision of footprints had battled amongst the dirt, ending as the bare footprints disappeared and were overtaken solely by the booted prints that disappeared when they reached the distant tree line.

The Indian warrior bent down and examined the ground with his fingers. He then scooped up a bit of dirt in his hands and sniffed it.

Tossing it down immediately, he muttered under his breath, "Cursed Kiawas!"

Charlie was nearly frantic. Kneeling beside his brother, he clutched at his hair in grief and fear.

"What shall we do?" he sputtered weakly.

"We shall punish them, of course." And with that, the chief placed a comforting arm around his younger brother.

Mackenzie Makes His Next Moves

As the sun crested the horizon, the last vestiges of night retreated behind a callous man. The brilliant blues of the first-lit sky met golden land. Cold retreated with the darkness and the chill in the air became refreshing. The scent of dew and grasses mixed with flowers in the cool breeze.

Mackenzie stood staring into the morning mists as they slowly dissipated from the high plains. It was a majestic sight. It felt to him as if he were standing on the edge of a great lake as the fog burned off. This lake was of land, although at some point in history it had been covered by a great inland sea.

That didn't matter now as he waited for his men to return. What was important was the success of their mission, and the anxiety in the soldier was apparent. As he paced the small stretch of ground, he constantly glanced toward the distant hills in hopes of spotting the returning scouting party.

What began as a modest cloud of dust slowly became a small group of riders making their way to the camp. They trotted gradually toward the waiting commander in a line of five horses.

From a distance it was difficult to tell if they had succeeded, but as Mackenzie held his field glass to his eye he could see the smiles on their faces. One of the riders appeared to have something slung across the rear of his horse. It was not moving of its own accord, but was swaying with the movement of the horse. It seemed to have arms and legs and long hair.

The horsemen rode into the camp and reined up in front of Mackenzie. Corporal Dan leaped from his horse with a flourish and bowed low, sweeping his hat across his body in a mock show of chivalry.

"I was successful, Colonel!"

"So I see…"

"It was easy, I tell you! Why, we just swept into the camp and made off with the squaw! I don't think anyone even noticed us!" Dan couldn't help but crow in delight as he lowered the prisoner to the ground in a sitting position, her hands and feet bound, and a rag tied about her mouth.

Mackenzie bent his chin into his gloved, three-fingered hand as he fell into deep thought. His subordinate waited patiently, but the grimace on his face spoke volumes. The other soldiers sat in silence, looking on in expectation of their next orders.

For several moments, it seemed as if the Colonel had fallen asleep standing there. As the troops became restless and the horses shuffled nervously, he awoke from his near-dream state. His movements indicated he had decided on his next move.

With the air of command that came naturally to him, he explained his plans to his chief subordinates, who would arrange the troops for what was to come.

When he finished, he asked his men, "All clear?"

"Yessir!" came the unanimous response.

There was one there who could not respond, yet heard the plan nonetheless. Little Wing struggled quietly against her bonds as she frantically tried to think of a way to escape and warn her people.

Leaving the Back Door Open

Charlie reigned up at the edge of the Cap Rock that overlooked the Fourth Cavalry encampment and frowned. Quanah pulled up on his Palomino and looked down. It immediately became clear that they were expected. Soldiers manned a series of trenches on two sides of the base. One of the sides abutted the cliff face and the fourth was enclosed by a stream. It was an exceedingly strong position, but lacked two features that would have made it ideal for a battle—a means of retreat and some way to counterattack if the opportunity presented itself. If the trenches were taken, the soldiers would be backed up against the cliff and creek with no way to escape.

This fact struck the two Indian leaders as strange. Typically, a US Army detachment, especially one led by such an astute captain as Mackenzie, would not have overlooked this glaring fault in the ground it had chosen for an engagement.

Another anomaly was the obvious reduction in number of men. There had been about twice as many bluecoats present during the Comanche's last fight. These soldiers could have been sent elsewhere or back to the reservation.

"Hmmm," Quanah said quietly. "Many less men."

"I noticed it too," Charlie stated as he shaded his eyes from the rising sun.

"Bad sign."

"Yes. Should we head back?"

"We are here. They are there. We attack."

Charlie Bird nodded, although he was thinking of the village they had left behind and the strange positioning of the enemy soldiers. He shook the feeling off and joined the other warriors in preparation to send the white men running for their lives.

Surprise Attack

Watching from his clifftop perch, Lieutenant Dan smiled as he witnessed the Comanche warriors file out of their camp in a neat line of horsemen. Resplendent in their black and red war-paint, they seemed like the very angels of battle. Each carried a rifle and a long, feather-decorated spear. Some had headdresses and others wore simple bands. Their leather-skinned trousers were perfect for riding and most wore no shirt. They rode with the horsemanship of people born to the saddle, becoming one with their mounts. Tall, short, broad, or slender, they all shared a common look of fierce determination.

Motioning to his men to remain hidden, Dan crept down from his vantage point to ready his men to attack the now nearly defenseless Comanche encampment with its population of women, children, and old men. He would visit upon them the same treatment they had meted out to countless white settlements. There would be no mercy.

"OK men. Here is our chance! We can wipe these heathens from the face of the earth! We must be strong! We must be resolute! We must be true to our duty!"

After a hushed cheer from the men, he explained the plan. It was simple, yet bound to be effective against the small resistance they would face. The troop would split up, with half proceeding to the south and the remainder approaching from the north. Thus surrounded on two sides and pressed up against the river, the only escape for the fleeing enemy would be to the west across the open plain, where they would be easy pickings for the well-equipped horsemen of the Fourth Cavalry Regiment.

The only question was whether Mackenzie could hold the Comanche warriors long enough for the other half of his command to destroy the Indian encampment and then come back to the aid of those holding the Native princess. There was a real possibility that one half would be destroyed, which would force the other to make a roundabout march of hundreds of miles to the nearest fort and safety. But war was about risk, and those who were boldest often prevailed.

Taking one last look at his men, Dan swung himself onto his horse and rode to the head of the troops.

"Remember, my fine fellows! No quarter!" he shouted as he dug his stirrups into his steed and charged down the hill toward the sleeping Comanche village. The soldiers streamed after him, hurrahing and brandishing their weapons.

An ancient squaw who was collecting water at the edge of the stream squinted through hanging skin at the dust and soldiers and prayed to the maker that her end would be quick.

Beginning the Game

Taking careful aim at a blue-coated soldier, Charlie squeezed his trigger gently. The unfortunate man dropped to the ground and the battle began in earnest as the Indians swept down from the cliff. The air was filled with whoops and battle cries and bullets.

The Indians rushed forward with abandon, spears held high. The neat line of attackers quickly became knots of warriors moving forward as Comanches stopped to reload before continuing down the precipice.

Reaching the bottom of the canyon, they rushed in a misaligned group toward the army position.

After the first rush of attack, the United States soldiers dove for their prearranged positions. Their rifles had been stacked ahead of time and each trench supplied with ample ammunition. Exposing less than a third of their bodies from the foxholes, their directed fire took a heavy toll on the charging Native Americans.

Gaining confidence in the effect of their fire and encouragement from Mackenzie—who was walking along the lines exhorting his men to take careful aim and conserve their ammunition—the soldiers began to hurrah.

The deep cheer that rose from the trenches mingled with the strident calls of the attacking Comanches to create a cacophony augmented by the screams of the wounded and pinging of bullets.

Many of the attackers lay sprawled in front of the trenches, dead or dying. The Indians reeled back, shocked by the stiff resistance and deadly rain of lead they were facing. All seemed lost for the Indians after just a few moments of the conflict.

As desperation crept into their thoughts, Quanah leapt to the cusp of a trench and, raising his rifle for all to see, roared with all his might. That inarticulate sound was like a rallying cry for his warriors, and they charged the soldiers once again.

There is a fierce fighting spirit that manifests itself in the hearts of those defending their homelands, and this provided an intangible advantage for the Comanches as they began to force their way into the ranks of the enemy. Hacking away at the first rank, the Native Americans began to make way and drive their opponents further back into their protective pits.

"All men must stand their ground!" Mackenzie bellowed above the din. With lifted sword in one hand and smoking pistol in the other, he charged headlong into the melee.

Complete Destruction

Dan raised his pistol to end one more Indian life, but then lowered it.

The old man was cowering in front of him, positively groveling. Dan thought he might have felt something akin to pity, deep down.

The Native was shouting something unintelligible to the army officer in the Comanche dialect. He looked to be begging for his life.

Dan contemplated what it would mean to save this savage's life, didn't think it worth the trouble, and killed him right there. Before the body hit the earth, he turned and rode off a bit to where his men were mopping up the last of the Indian encampment.

Bodies lay scattered about in various degrees of anguish and smoke rose acrid in the morning air. Teepees had been trampled and tipped over and most of the buffalo meat had been thrown into the nearby creek, which had turned a sickening red hue.

"Well sir," a sergeant stated matter-of-factly, "we're done here. There's nothing left to destroy."

"Yes, it appears so, Sergeant. Round up the men at the pass there. We're only half done with our mission."

"Trap some Indians, sir?"

"Got that right. Now get going! We've no time to waste!"

"Yessir!"

"Oh, one last thing," the commanding officer called after his subordinate.

"Sir?"

"Burn the teepees and shoot all of their horses. They won't be needing them anymore."

"Sir!"

Shortly, there was a column of smoke rising pall-like into the midday sky.

Before joining his men sitting their horses in a blue knot, Dan turned once more to view the destruction he and his men had wrought. It was indeed complete. He couldn't help but smile, and the morning light glinted off his gold tooth.

Biding Time

Watching from a distance was Little Wing. She sat, hands tied behind her back, propped against a wagon as the battle unfolded fifty feet below and a hundred yards in front.

She had been kept prisoner in Mackenzie's headquarters wagon. The army chieftain had treated her well, keeping her fed. He had even let her wander about a bit, although constantly under guard.

The Indian princess had been staring off at where she supposed her tribe would be when she noticed something move. It may have been her imagination, but she knew better. Little Wing knew her people would never let her stay captive for long. That hint of movement was the beginning of the rescue effort.

Now that the battle had erupted in all its fury, she wondered what she should do. Glancing left, it became apparent that the guard was just as occupied with the battle as his captive. Now may be her time to escape. As she was about to run, the guard glanced back at her. She thought better of it and sat back down to await a better opportunity.

It All Comes Crashing...

While the fight was raging, Charlie made his way around the battlefield searching for his love. After firing his first shot, he skirted the rocks and boulders toward the bottom of the defile. Reaching the bottom, he crawled through the waving grass as stray bullets whizzed by overhead.

He spied a knoll upon which sat a wagon that looked to belong to someone of importance. There, at least, was a place to start his search.

Approaching the hillock was no easy matter as it was firmly in enemy hands. Projectiles screamed through the air, striking ground and kicking up spurts of dust all around.

Charlie kept low as he ran from cover to cover. Once, a shot passed so close to his head that he could smell the gunpowder. After many such near misses, he reached the foot of the elevation and looked up.

Atop the hill was a sentry. Clear against the blue sky, he stood. When the opportunity presented itself, he'd raise his rifle and pull off a shot, then lower the rifle and smile with satisfaction as the bullet hit home and another enemy was vanquished.

This erstwhile sniper was tasked with guarding the Indian princess, who was the immediate cause of the commotion. He was clearly not focused on his assignment, but rather on taking pot shots. Despite the fact of his inattention, he still presented a formidable obstacle between Little Wing and her savior.

Charlie was an avenging angel and rescuer wrapped into one, and as the fight rose in intensity to his left, he slowly inched his way up the slope through the chaparral that ringed the hill. Thorns dug into his skin and scraped at his knees. He became one with the surroundings and, although the din would have prevented his being heard, he accomplished his ascent in silence.

Just as Charlie Bird crested the edge of the plateau that formed the top of the elevation, the guard turned to adjust his gun strap, his gaze falling on the black-faced warrior who seemed to have appeared from nowhere.

Their eyes locked for a moment and then, realizing the peril to his charge, the guard, whose name was Tom, ran back to Little Wing. She had taken full advantage of the momentary shock to free herself of her bonds and was now clambering down the slope, away from the battle. Tom leapt down the hill in hot pursuit with Charlie Bird following close behind, knife drawn.

Little Wing tripped over a protuberance close to the bottom of the knoll and rolled forward. She attempted to regain her footing, but the soldier caught her by the neck and swung her about to face the hill she had just tumbled down.

Now, holding Little Wing with his arm around her neck, Tom was able to take stock of his situation. He was about a hundred yards from the command wagon atop the elevation, which was about thirty feet above. The knoll blocked the battle from view but not from sound as the air was filled with the screams of the wounded, rifle fire from both sides, and cannons from the US Army. His attention was focused not on the fight, which he could not see, but on Charlie Bird, the black-faced savage Native warrior with heaving chest and dripping knife drawn.

"Me no hurt her! You leave now! You no leave, I kill her!" Tom shouted at his enemy.

Charlie rolled his eyes and spoke clearly, "I speak English perfectly, you fool. Let the girl go!"

"And if I don't?" The question hung there.

"Well then, my blue-coated friend, I'll just have to kill you and take her back. Either way, I'll get her back. It's a question of whether you want to live to see another South-Western sunrise. I'll give you ten seconds to think about it." And with that, the warrior calmly sat down, cross-legged, as if he were enjoying a day in the park.

The soldier was trembling now. The offhand way with which the Indian had spoken was more unsettling than if his opponent had been ranting and raving in anger. Tom had to think quickly if he was to get out of this scrape. If he let the Indian princess go, he'd be court-martialed or shot by Mackenzie. The army had no patience for incompetence these days, and he'd witnessed plenty of men sent to their Maker for lesser offenses than letting a captive escape. On the other hand, he could kill the squaw and take his chances with this savage warrior and his excellent elocution. That didn't seem to have a positive outcome; he'd surely lose. A third possibility presented itself to his frantic mind. He could keep the young lady as a hostage and thereby be allowed back to the wagon and safety. This Indian brave may be a skilled and practiced warrior, but he would never risk harming the lady he was so concerned for.

Tom was just about to call out to the Indian something to the effect of his keeping the hostage until he was safely back, when he was cut short by a knife flying into his forehead. He stumbled back, releasing his captive and then fell back dead among the brambles, the blade's handle sticking up toward the sky.

"Eleven," Charlie counted. "You waited too long to make up your mind."

Little Wing remained motionless, stunned for a moment before Charlie ran to her and swept her up in an embrace. The reunion only lasted a moment, though. Danger was all around them and they needed to find safety quickly.

Charlie held her at arm's length and spoke softly, "I don't know what I'd have done if he had harmed you! It's my fault you are here at all. I should have guarded you better!"

"No, Charlie Bird! You've done everything you could have! And you saved me yet again! You will always protect me; we will raise a family and live in peace!"

Charlie looked down at the ground. "We have much to accomplish before that happens. For now, let us leave this place!"

Little Wing looked deeply into his eyes and nodded, as if to say, "I will follow you anywhere!"

Just then, her eyes widened as her gaze became fixed over her betrothed's shoulder.

"Charlie!" she screamed and jumped around him, quick as lightning. A shot rang out and she crumpled to the ground.

Charlie whirled around in time to see Mackenzie lower his rifle. His grin was replaced by a look of shock as the result of his shot became apparent. Then, shrugging off the fact that he had just killed the young lady, he lifted the gun to his shoulder once more— this time to finish the job.

At that very moment, an arrow sliced through the smoky air. With an audible "thwack" it embedded itself in Mackenzie's shoulder. He groaned in pain and grasped the wounded shoulder, letting his gun drop.

Charlie swept Little Wing's crumpled form from the blood-dampened earth and rushed off without looking back; she seemed light as a feather.

Finding a safer spot, he lay his love down gently and took stock of her injury. It was clearly serious and the princess squeezed her eyes in silent agony. She uttered not a word.

The blood seeping from her mouth mixed with Charlie's tears as he beheld her slipping away. Her breaths became shallow and her eyes opened, although they were fixed on nothing.

Charlie frantically searched her abdomen, looking for the bullet. It had been of large caliber and lodged itself somewhere deep inside her body. As he investigated the wound, it became apparent that massive damage had been done. She was bleeding profusely from the gash in her torso.

The wound was so serious that the sorrowful warrior had not the slightest idea how to save her. He cradled her head in his lap and looked for help from the G-d he never thought of anymore.

Her lovely eyes regained their focus for a moment and she looked at her husband-who-would-never-be with sadness and fear. She opened her mouth and pronounced in a barely audible voice, "Do not cry, my Charlie Bird. Find someone to make you happy!"

"It is only you, Little Wing!" he cried.

Her body went limp in Charlie's arms and he looked to the heavens, screamed his warrior's scream, and cried.

Charlie Bird pounded his fist on his thigh in impotent rage. His first thoughts were of his loss. Those were crowded from his mind by something else. Vengeance. This he swore he would have.

Up In Smoke

Surrounded and in dire straits, all Indian organization fell apart within minutes and the warriors dashed pell-mell from the battlefield.

Mackenzie, an arrow lodged in his shoulder, was carried off in severe pain having carried out his goal of tamping down Comanche resistance. His embarrassment at his carelessness of exposing his own person on that hilltop in trying to kill his nemesis would haunt him until his last day.

Quanah Parker fought like a demon that day, tossing American soldiers like rag dolls and sparing none. His presence alone was enough to keep his forces fighting with fierce determination.

Although the nomadic Comanche nation would linger on for three more years, that day marked the death knell of their three-hundred-year-old dominance of the Southern Plains.

The United States Army held its position for another hour until Lieutenant Dan and his men descended on the Indian rear with a ferocious surprise assault.

The column of smoke that rose from the destruction of the Comanche camp was like the last gasp of a dying warrior: Final.

3. New Beginnings

The Arrival

The young woman in seat seven-B of the third car wiped her face with a kerchief. It was much hotter in Missouri than it was back east. The air was heavy, and the motion of the locomotive and small vent in the car did little to alleviate the congested, humid feeling in the air. Other passengers were likewise wiping their brows and faces or fanning themselves in futile attempts to stave off the vexing heat.

Rebecca replaced the damp cloth in her handbag and looked out the window as the telegraph poles shot by in a blur. After passing through Toledo, Ohio, the scenery had turned decidedly rural, with farms and farm houses dotting the scenery as far as the eye could see. The track clung tightly to the edge of the Missouri River for a time and then turned North as it made its way through the second growth timber and brush of the Missouri countryside. Fields of rolling green separated by clumps of trees began to appear, and a fringe of willow trees filled the horizon.

Just as the locomotive broke through the trees, the sun peaked out from behind the clouds and bathed the entire scene in warm afternoon light. The train blew its whistle as it crossed the mighty Missouri River on a trestle bridge. The river was wide at this point, and the brown water rose and fell in waves from the various steamers that wound their way toward the confluence with the Mississippi some hundred miles east.

Rebecca turned from the spectacular scene and rummaged through her bag for a moment. Finding the piece of paper she was looking for, she carefully unfolded it and spread it on her lap.

Dr. Richards had told her to look for his agent, Mr. Cosworth. He was the representative who would accompany her to her new position as the sole teacher and headmistress at the newly established school on the Kiowa, Apache, and Comanche Reservation.

She blew out a nervous breath as she thought of that misty day in New York several months before when she had first noticed the man dressed as an Indian holding a sign that said "Teachers Wanted!"

The advertising trick had worked and Rebecca, along with several other young women, had run down from one of the surrounding tenements to hear what this "chief" had to say.

It turned out to be exactly what she'd been looking for and it had come none too soon. The money she had saved in Philadelphia before traveling to New York was nearly gone and she had been working for pennies, not covering her rent, and starving from lack of food. In another few weeks, she would have had to return to her parents' home and admit defeat, her dream of teaching the less-privileged relegated to the dustbin of her life.

This opportunity, although dangerous, was full of adventure, challenge, and the promise of doing good. The Quakers, a peaceful people who felt it was their duty to make the world a better place, had taken up the challenge of "civilizing" the savage red man by opening schools for the Plains Natives with the government's blessing. They needed teachers, of course, and that meant seeking out young, talented, ideological women with little or no connections keeping them at home.

Rebecca fit the profile to a T.

The crowd of women had thinned considerably after hearing what the teaching was all about, and then after the interviews had been conducted in a dingy restaurant on the Lower East Side of

Manhattan, there were but five candidates left. They were given the choice of going to one of several reservations, and Rebecca chose the most wild sounding. She figured that as long as she was going through with this, she should go all the way.

That was how she found herself on the train bound for Columbia, Missouri, and then by buggy to Franklin, whence the Santa Fe Trail began. She would traverse the Great Plains in a wagon train before reaching the reservation to meet her charges. What would they be like? Would they be the uncouth savages to be tamed that she'd read about in the newspapers, or would they be little angels she could mold and shape into models of society? Only time would tell.

The steam engine drew up beside the station amidst a swirl of coal smoke and jerked to a halt. The conductor made his way down the aisle shouting, "Last stop! Columbia! Last Stop!"

Taking a deep breath she stood up, ready to exit the train.

Rebecca and Cosworth

Rebecca jumped down with a youthful energy from the train and began searching for her contact. His name was Mr. Ezra Cosworth and she hoped he'd be a pleasant traveling companion; she would have to spend over a week with him as she made her way along the Santa Fe trail toward her final destination.

Looking about, she found several men who held promise but they all passed her by, casting glances at her extreme beauty but making no sign of recognition.

About to give up, she scanned the platform once more and recognized her patron. She winced involuntarily as she walked toward the elderly gentleman who was waving his straw hat.

He had the look of the typical country politician, all jovial bluster and good nature overlying a selfishness and sliminess that showed through his exterior to all but the most dull-witted observer. He was grossly overweight and sweating profusely through his blue linen shirt. A thin film of moisture clung to his brow while his florid cheeks puffed up unhealthily with every exhalation of breath.

"Ah, my lady! I'm Mr. Cosworth with the Bureau of Indian Affairs. I'll accompany you on your way to the reservation and make sure that you get settled in all right."

"A pleasure to meet you, sir." She lightly grasped the hand proffered.

"I see you've found the trip not too hard! You look positively spritely!"

"Yes, it was all in all a comfortable trip," she replied after a slight hesitation.

"Well then," he continued, "I'll just have the porter take your bags. Where is your baggage ticket?"

"I have none. This," she said as she pointed at the suitcase she had put down at her side, "is all I've got."

A look of astonishment crossed his florid face for a moment before he resumed his fixed, insincere smile.

"This should be easy enough, then."

Turning, Cosworth addressed his Native American aide, who amounted to little more than a servant, "Robert! Please take the young lady's bag!"

Returning his somewhat lurid gaze to the young lady in his presence, he extended his arm in a friendly fashion.

"Come, my dear! We are off to educate the Comanches!"

Hiring A Guide

Rebecca gripped her bag tightly as the wagon rumbled into Franklin, Missouri. This dusty little town was the famous Santa Fe trailhead. Nearly all traffic that traveled to the important trading post of Santa Fe, New Mexico started at the inconspicuous marker wherefrom it led southwest into some of the wildest country the United States had to offer.

A guide swaggered over to the pretty young woman escorted by a balding man who was sweating profusely in the midday sun. Cosworth fanned himself every so often with his straw hat before placing it back on his shining pate.

A rude population had settled there to take care of the travelers' needs and outfitting for the arduous nine-hundred-mile trek. Crude stores boasted wares such as tents, provisions, horseshoes, and wagon wheels, while other such truck held within them crafty types whose prices changed depending on the desperation and apparent intelligence of the customer. There were the bars and taverns whose goods and offerings appealed to the baser instincts of the excursionists preparing for their journeys.

Lastly, there were the guides. A class of wild men who loved adventure more than safety. Having spent years living and fighting in the west, these hardened men sported waxed mustaches and chaps. Their dusty boots had shining silver spurs. Most of them did anyway, as they were prone to showmanship. Some of the best riders and surest shots served the public in this way.

The price for their service was high, yet mostly worth it. If ever one found oneself in a tight scrape, these guides were worth their weight in gold. Brave to a fault, they would perform the most amazing deeds when their charges were confronted with hostile Indians, bandits and the like.

These actions grew to superhuman accomplishments by the time the stories were told and retold in some western saloon. These men were said to roast rattlesnakes with lightning bolts for dinner and finish them off with swigs of turpentine. And, best of all, people believed it. Everyone loves a hero.

"Now what brings a delicate little lady such as yourself to a hole such as Franklin?" the guide drawled as he twirled his mustache around a brown finger. His English was excellent, with only a hint of a Mexican accent around the edges of his words.

The bald man spoke first. "We're heading down to the reservation in Oklahoma. She's going to teach the savages and I'm her escort. Name's Fred. Fred Thompson." He held out a pudgy hand.

"That so?" the guide murmured.

Still twisting his mustache, he gave them each a once-over with a practiced eye and then stated matter-of-factly, "Guess you'll be needing a guide."

Thompson shook his head vigorously and exclaimed, "Why yes, we do, and I've got the full backing of the US government. If you can get us to our destination safely, I assure you the pay will be quite adequate!"

Rebecca had remained silent as this exchange was taking place. She felt rather uncomfortable at the unabashed way with which the guide looked at her. A quick glance of attraction was one thing, but this man did nothing to hide his thoughts and it made her queasy.

"Well then," she began with an air of nonchalance, "we should agree to terms and be on our way. The children will need to start school as soon as possible."

The guide smiled in agreement and then said, after a brief pause, "I agree with Ms.... Ah, I don't believe I've had the honor of knowing your name yet."

"Ms. Katz," she stated drily. "And your name is?"

He bowed with some flourish, tipping his hat in the process.

"Don Carlos Santos is my given name, but my friends call me Doc on account of my excellent education." He winked at the lady as he said this, and the sun glinted off his gold tooth.

Rebecca turned away with barely disguised repugnance, although Thompson seemed elated to have found a well-spoken man as a guide.

"Let us proceed to make an agreement then," the older man stated gleefully. "I believe this restaurant will have a table for us to get out of the heat and discuss the finalization of our trip!"

With that, the government representative lumbered off toward the door of a nearby saloon with Rebecca following, her nose in the air. Don Carlos "Doc" Santos shrugged to himself and followed the pair into the cool confines of the dining establishment.

Rebecca sat across from Don Santos, the prospective guide, in the dark, dusty bar. A man at the piano pounded out some jaunty tune that was not in keeping with the atmosphere as a woman in a red dress leaned on the piano, feigning interest in the music. Light from a broken window streamed in through the smoke-filled air and a musty smell pervaded the space. Combined with whiskey and a lady's perfume, it formed a tantalizing, yet somewhat lurid mix. It was all very new to the teacher from back east, and she folded her arms a bit tighter in an attempt to distance herself from the alien surroundings.

Her traveling companion seemed quite at home as he discussed the proposition of travel excitedly with the insolent guide.

"It's just a matter of waiting a few weeks and lining the right pockets, if you know what I mean. You'll get there safe and sound with no fuss," the guide was saying.

"Yes, of course. This is a government concern, you know, and I've got the full backing of the US Department of Indian Affairs Agency behind me."

That really seemed to hit home with Santos and his eyes lit up briefly.

"Well, of course you do," he smiled, hiding an avaricious grin beneath his black moustache.

"Yes, indeed! I can pay whatever you feel is necessary to ensure our safe travel! How much do you figure, Mr. Santos?"

The man tipped his head back in thoughtful repose for a moment. It was almost comical, as anyone except for the agency man could have seen that Don Santos was already spending the windfall that fate seemed to have dumped right into his lap.

Mr. Cosworth sat with a silly grin and sipped at his whiskey, which had already been paid for by the guide.

Rebecca was growing impatient with the desire to be quit of the place, so she clucked her tongue derisively.

"What's the little lady getting on about?" Santos asked, turning his attention once again to the young lady sitting across from him.

"It's very apparent you'll be paid well for your efforts, sir, so let us get on with it!" she exclaimed, in the most sour tone she could muster.

The usually confident guide was taken aback by an affront to his supposed charms. He simply narrowed his eyes and smiled more broadly at the woman. His look was returned with just as much disdain—or maybe even more.

"Yes, well…" Mr. Cosworth coughed a bit, breaking up the icy exchange. "I think we should be getting packed and ready for the trip."

As the teacher and her traveling companion rose from the table, the young lady remembered something she'd heard back east. "Have you heard anything of the Indian raids? We've been reading of them recently. Have they ceased to happen?"

"Oh yes, my good lady," he answered, offering an exaggerated courtesy. "They most certainly have. As long as we know who to speak to with this," he added, rubbing his thumb and forefinger together with the universal sign for money, "it shouldn't be a problem!"

Charlie's Rogues

Cleaning his knife had taken on a significance all its own. It was no longer a chore for Charlie Bird. Rather, it was symbolic. Wiping the blood from the blade meant that another foe had been vanquished, yet it was more than that. It was one step closer to the revenge he sought from the world. In his eyes, the world, fate or whomever was responsible for his current state surely owed him at least some succor for the pain.

Quanah had taken the high road, figuring everything that had happened was due to some fate or destiny manifesting itself in time. Perhaps that was too philosophical for one as pragmatic as the Comanche warrior chief. Nevertheless, Parker had not taken part in the brutal raids that his adopted brother led across the Texas plains. He felt that such actions, aside from being morally unjust and uncalled for, would lead to a much quicker end for the Comanche people.

He knew that the continued depredations would bring out the United States Army in all its military might. And these were men to be feared. They made no distinctions between warriors and non-combatants, old and young, men and women, fighters and peacemakers. The fight against the Indian would be brought to a final conclusion, and the question was how disadvantageous that finale would be for the former rulers of the southern plains, the Comanche.

If the current outrage against the Texas wagon trains and settlers didn't cease soon, any free Indian on the plains would be forcibly dealt with and the winter rations the US government handed out to those residing on the reservations would be held until the people were no more.

Therefore, in the interests of his people, Quanah had to locate Charlie and the band of malcontents he had gathered and bring them to bay. The task was easier planned than carried out however, and he knew his brother would not lie down without a fight. He had taught Charlie the ways of war, and perhaps the younger man knew them just as well as his older brother. Perhaps better.

Charlie Bird now found himself hunted by not only the United States Army, but his own kith and kin as well. He had become a pariah. This mattered not to him, as he only sought revenge as the salve to his wounds. A way to bring the world the type of pain he was feeling, and perhaps bring it all crashing down on his head.

How was it that people could pursue altruistic motives and good deeds when the next second some heinous act could bring it all to an end—especially when the very people one hoped to save now hoped for one's destruction as well?

These were Charlie's thoughts as he stood from cleaning his blade and approached his men as they sat by the fire.

"Boys," he said, using the word as one would affectionately call to his childhood friends. "We have a ranch to visit this night. It is well away from others and full of horses and cattle. There may be a guard or two, but when has this stopped us before?"

The others nodded silently. They were stoic, yet inwardly excited at the prospect of mischief. Each of them had their own stories and reasons for joining the band that had struck terror in the hearts of people across the Texas panhandle and beyond.

There was Big Bear, whose family had been separated and then enslaved by the white man down in New Mexico. He was perhaps the largest and strongest of the group, dwarfing any horse he rode. His fierce determination to avenge his loved ones was only matched by his fierceness in battle.

Pahayoko, whose name meant "amorous one," was anything but romantic in his bloodthirsty behavior toward all settlers. He was of immense strength and heavy shoulder, but crippled in his gait, almost simian in his movements. He had been slighted at a trade fair many years ago and then accosted by a rowdy gang of bandits, tortured, and left for dead among the crags of the Cap Rock.

Upon waking, he had crawled many miles to his camp only to find that the robbers had murdered his comrades and plundered their belongings. He had not had the strength to eat nor drink and had fallen asleep amongst his dead brothers. He had later been found by a passing Indian band and nursed back to health.

His mental state had never quite returned and he had spent the past several years living as a wild animal amongst the hills. He never cooked the meat he ate and snarled unintelligibly when approached by strangers. Charlie Bird had discovered him one night scavenging for food. When asked if he wanted to join Charlie in taking the starch out of the white man, he had become suddenly sane and joined right up. One thing was certain in his crippled mind, and that was his thirst for revenge against light-skinned people. They were all evil to him.

"Up! To the trail!" Charlie said, smiling wickedly as the firelight flickered before him, sending shadows across his strong face.

He suddenly looked skyward, turning his head to the rising moon. As he did so, a tear rolled down his cheek. Little Wing was there somewhere with him. Perhaps she was happy; perhaps not. Either way, her pain was no longer hers. He would bear it for the both of them. For that, he could smile.

The Journey Begins

The coyote howled and bid farewell to the night. A clock had chimed five times and the first bits of light were beginning to outline the distant hills. The revelers had long since shuffled off either in groups or singly to sleep off the excesses of the evening.

One arm stretched across the table in the murky darkness of the saloon. The man's moustache moved rhythmically with every breath. Don Carlos groaned and attempted to lift a head that felt as heavy as lead. It was no use. The alcohol was too much, even for one as experienced in its consumption as he. This new gig he had found suited him just fine with its five dollars per week pay and other, less tangible benefits. One of those benefits—he had to admit—was the company, albeit reluctantly kept, of the beautiful Rebecca Katz.

This G-d forsaken hole of a town was an unpolished and filthy setting for a gem of the first order like the young Miss Katz. Sure, he got how someone would want to make a difference, but educating the savages was not on his short list of worthwhile things to do. Why she would waste her time pursuing such a task while risking life and limb, when she could be the debutante or the belle of any society she wanted back east, was beyond his ability to understand.

Ah well! She *was* here, and it was his job to make sure she got to where she was going safely. The US government was her backer and they paid well indeed! Don Carlos would do his best to make sure he carried out his mission as expertly as he had handled past jobs of this nature.

Right now though, he had to make sure he didn't spin off the table his black-maned head was resting on. More time for thought of higher complexity in the morning. Now, he would rest a bit more in preparation for the long journey they would all begin that day.

"Get up, you sot!" she said through clenched teeth as she kicked the chair out from underneath him. He crashed to the floor like a puppet whose strings had been cut.

A searing sunbeam caught him on the right cheek as he cracked open his eye. It took a moment for the world to come into focus. The pain in his head reminded him of the excesses of the night before. Had he really bought drinks for the house? Where was his money anyway? Who was this lovely lady scowling down at him?

A smile creased his weather-beaten countenance as he remembered.

"Up, you imbecile!" she seethed. "We are late to begin and it's your fault! I should have known you'd be here! Now let's go!"

Don Carlos stood unsteadily and adjusted his hat. Feeling his pockets for his gun and finding it, he shook his head to clear the cobwebs.

"Wow! Did you get the number on that train?" he muttered.

"The wagon train is leaving, you drunk! Let's go!" She huffed out through the saloon doors and walked briskly toward a smiling—and always sweating—Mr. Cosworth.

"Coming, lady," he said, unable to keep from smiling to himself. He stumbled toward the achingly bright entrance. This would prove to be *some* interesting journey, of that he was sure. Little did he know, however, just how prescient his thoughts that morning would be.

The Trail Is No Place to Let Your Guard Down

He washed his face in the acrid water of the stream that wound its way from the angles and outcroppings of the Cap Rock. It had been weeks and very little indication of the girl or her captors. She must be this way, though. He'd heard tell of the Comanche tribes living out this way. How had he wound up beaten, bedraggled, and hungry here in no man's land?

It had all begun on one horrible night some two weeks before.

Don Carlos had been traveling along the Santa Fe Trail as he was accustomed to do, leading the wagon train headed through Comanche country. He had been making a special trip to drop off Rebecca Katz, the teacher, at the Indian reservation when the trouble began.

The teams had stopped for the evening. The heat had come down and a crackling fire sent smoke into the crisp, starlit night air. The smell from the sizzling buffalo meat was intoxicating to all who were gathered for the evening repast.

Don Carlos called in the guards to eat. He supposed that no Indian would attack so early in the evening. They usually waited until the night was mostly over so that most of the camp would be sleeping. Everyone was well armed, so he wasn't afraid. He should have known the situation would be different now, what with the Indian bands scattered and that rogue Comanche group already having burned another wagon train a week ago.

Rebecca had gotten used to trail life with its rough, jostling rides in stifling desert heat. The humor of the men was equally rough, but they were gentlemen and treated her like the lady she was. Even Don Carlos had been reserved, in his own way.

Her government escort was a different matter entirely. Mr. Cosworth's constitution was familiar with Eastern city foods and did not take kindly to the grub of the Western environs. He spent quite a bit of time in the brush beside the road performing the "Texas Two Step," as the crew jokingly referred to the relief associated with stomach issues.

His color had grown noticeably paler and he would not leave the wagon except for his urgent personal needs, even during the cooler morning hours. He lay there prostrate most of the day and night, clutching his midsection and moaning.

In the midst of his pain, he was aroused from a restive slumber by a faint sound, almost like the scratching of a stick on a rock. Cosworth turned to peer out the entrance of the wagon and saw the stars forming a shining necklace across the dark blanket of sky. Suddenly, something slightly darker than the night eclipsed part of the opening and sprouted a pair of white eyes, which glared maliciously at the open-mouthed sick man lying there.

The invalid tried to scream, but his voice was hoarse and weak from his illness. The government emissary could only whimper as the Indian closed his hand over his victim's mouth.

More shadows appeared in the night and quietly surrounded the unsuspecting members of the caravan. Two broke off for the herd of horses and untied them with a deftness that could only have been achieved through a lifetime of dealing with ponies.

As the remuda was led off into the night, the Indians crept closer to the unsuspecting travelers. The leader of the warriors let out the most spine-tingling howl that any of the whites had ever heard, freezing each in his place.

That call was the signal for the attack. Tomahawks and arrows came flying in. One buried itself in the cook's back and he fell over screaming into the pot of food he had been tending to.

As the Indians closed around the circle, the trailblazers ran for their guns and did what they could to protect themselves. The Natives had painted themselves black against the night and their forms flitted across the moonlit night like so many shadows.

It was a forgone conclusion as to who would win this fight. Some of the hands ducked behind wagon wheels and knelt to shoot. Defense was an exercise in futility and several Americans fell screaming from the wounds inflicted by slashing axes and rifle shots.

Of the Indians, one was fiercer than the others, savagely hacking away at the fallen cowboys with his long knife. Grunting with the effort, he scalped one after another without waiting to see if they were dead. His bare chest was covered in blood as he rose from his latest victim.

He looked around in the chaos of the attack for his next quarry. His eyes fell on the tall lass with the rifle who was aiming as expertly as any of the men. She fired and reloaded the repeating gun. She appeared tough, but she was facing away from him and would be easy prey. He stalked forth like some horrible black spider, long legs scratching marks in the sandy earth, barely making a sound. He came close enough to strike and raised his knife with a wicked smile.

With a swift motion, he turned the lady with one arm, knocking her rifle to the ground. His other hand swept in a vicious arc to strike, but what was this?! A hand as powerful as his own grabbed his forearm and held it firmly in place. Turning his head menacingly to see what had prevented his latest kill, he came face to face with his leader, Charlie Bird.

"Pahayoko!" He screamed in the Comanche dialect. "Leave her! We will take her with us!"

"I don't care anything for her! Let me kill her and have her scalp!" the warrior screamed through clenched teeth.

"No! We do not kill women like that! Not in my band!"

"Ah, but you are a white man and have the white man's ways regarding women! Perhaps I am in the wrong band! Now, move before I strike you down too!"

"You know what will happen if you try!" Charlie said, his eye twitching ever so slightly. Yet he did not move. He held the other man in a gaze that could have frozen water. The meaning conveyed was clear.

Pahayoko seethed, his chest rising and falling. He thought for a moment and ceased to struggle, standing down. He sheathed his knife and stepped back.

"This is not over, my friend!" he uttered, before dashing into the darkness.

"Perhaps not," Charlie said, sighing as he turned toward the woman who was cowering on the earth next to a wagon wheel.

The young lady had witnessed the entire exchange between the two Indians, but had not understood a word. It sounded so much like grunting that she couldn't fathom why she'd been spared. She had been sure she'd be killed, scalped, and perhaps worse when the native had spun her around, shaking loose her rifle, which had clattered to the ground. Next thing she knew, another Indian had grabbed the first by the arm and prevented him from doing more harm.

The shock must have caused her to lose her mind! Was that English he was speaking?

"Get up, now! He is gone and you are safe!"

"Th-Th-Thank you!" she managed to sputter as she took the hand extended to her.

As she got up and brushed the dirt from her dress, Rebecca Katz got a good, long look at her savior.

Surveying the Damage - Action Taken

Don Carlos had been in a drunken stupor as soon as the first war whoop shattered the camp silence. That had sobered him up some and he'd run for the hills. Diving behind a berm, he was able to watch the battle without risking his own skin. He had seen a few others from the wagon train flit off into the night, but the majority of the party was caught in the melee.

The trail boss felt a twinge of guilt at not leading his party in battle, but the screams of the wounded combined with the flying arrows suppressed the feeling sufficiently to keep him hidden.

When the Indians had left the camp, all that was left was a smoking wreck of twisted wood and lifeless bodies. The rising pall reflected eerily in the moonlight and none of the usual sounds from the horses or camp talk permeated the silence.

Don Carlos sank down behind the dirt mound again to contemplate his situation. What should he do now? First thing would be to check the camp.

He'd start as soon as the sun came up. No telling what might be lurking in the dark over in the ravaged campsite. At least in the light he'd have a fair shot.

Shortly after sunrise, he made his way back to collect what supplies he could. There wasn't much there. What hadn't been stolen had been burned by the Indians. Then he noticed that a few stragglers had found their way back. One hunched over an injured man, holding his hand. As the hand went limp, the man looked up sorrowfully to see his trail boss standing there with his hands on his hips.

"He's gone, Carlos. They're all gone!" he exclaimed with a sweeping gesture toward the lifeless figures strewn about.

"So I see..." Don Carlos frowned.

The man began to whimper. "I was eating with Smith here last night. All was well. We were talking of sweethearts back home and..." The sobs absorbed his last words.

The guide suddenly slapped the crying man across the face. The bawling immediately ceased and was simultaneously replaced by a look of shock.

"No time for keening like an old woman, Jackson!" he yelled, stiffening up. "We will never get this straightened out if you keep up your crying! I've got to think, so shut up!"

The options that presented themselves did not appeal to him.

He could spend time looking for survivors, and perhaps if his charges, Rebecca Katz and Cosworth, were still among the living, he could continue the trek toward his final destination on foot—seeing as the horses had all been stolen.

Upon arrival, he might get his pay, but probably no recommendation from the US government; and he may even lose the reputation he had built as a trail leader.

Other than those choices, he figured he could make his way back to Franklin and claim that he'd been swamped by overwhelming numbers, and even though he had been careful enough—though he hadn't been—they'd gotten the better of him.

And then what if the lady made it back? She would spill the beans and he'd be done for. His career as a guide would end right then and there. No, that option was out.

He thought it better to go find the girl and her escort and make sure she never spoke about this affair again, either by convincing her to keep silent or by any other means necessary.

After a time, he spoke to his comrade. "Let us do a little search here and see who's still with us among the living."

Together they proceeded to check the wagons to see which of the party had survived. Don Carlos's interest at finding the woman was foremost in his mind.

"Well, we won't be finding Cosworth out on the plains," the trail man said after checking a smoking wagon.

"What do you mean? Maybe he fled."

"Look for yourself," he responded, while pointing at the wreckage.

Jackson slowly approached and peered inside. He gasped and withdrew, horror etched across his weather-beaten features.

"Oh my sweet Lord..." he said, then sank his voice to a whisper, "the brutes!"

"Yes, my friend, these Indians are none too kind when they go on a raid, are they?"

"I'll go to the fort! I will tell the army what happened here!" And with that, Jackson ran off into the tall grass.

"You fool! You'll never make it! It's..." But then Carlos thought better of it and fell silent. He was pretty sure Jackson wouldn't make it back—alive anyway—and maybe that was a good thing. The fewer people that knew what happened here, the better.

Carlos walked from the smoking skeleton and the wagons and cast his gaze across the barren landscape. Something caught his eye. A red scarf had been thrown across a bush about a hundred yards from the camp's destruction. She had left a signpost of sorts! His hand fell to his gun. The woman was out there somewhere, and he had to find her.

Safe?

Rebecca rode along through that night on the back of her savior's horse. She felt a strange mixture of fear and safety. This marauder had murdered on the spot. That was something. In fact, he'd saved her. She had actually been protected at substantial risk to his life.

There were two questions that brooked largest in her mind: Why had he saved her and where was he taking her?

She had always been one for the most direct route, so she spoke up from the back of the horse. "Why did you protect me... and where are we going?"

The man said nothing. He only looked back as they bumped along, with a look that scared her into silence.

She remained that way for a time as she thought about what was happening to her. A few minutes later, the memory of that threatening look had faded, so she asked again, this time with more force.

"I know you understand English. Please tell me why you saved me and where we are headed."

Again, she was greeted with the same look. The other braves riding with them glanced over in curiosity, but remained silent.

This was repeated a few more times until it became perfectly clear to Rebecca that she would get no answer out of the Indian.

Finally, after a few hours of travel, the sun began to peek its head above the horizon. The first shades of purple began to dispel the star-spangled darkness.

She was suddenly aware of how tired she was. She'd been hanging on for dear life to the horse as the Indian chief piloted it down ravines and up seemingly impassable cliff faces until they arrived on the high, grassy plains.

After a time—she wasn't sure how long—the group suddenly halted. As if by some hidden sign, they all descended from their mounts and began rummaging about in the darkness.

She was not offered a hand off the horse, so she remained on it, looking at the faces that flitted by in the moonlight for an indication of the intentions of these heathens who held her against her will. One fact she knew for certain was that if an opportunity for escape presented itself, she'd run. Better to take a chance out on the open plains than with these barbarians.

As if in response to her thoughts, the Indian who had saved her life whispered to her, "I wouldn't run if I were you. These friends of mine wouldn't let you get far, and I don't think I could protect you once they're let loose."

Rebecca turned to face the man with a look that bespoke shock. Her mouth opened to speak, but nothing came out.

"Name's Charlie," he spoke with a wink before walking back to his comrades, who were setting up a fire.

Quanah Meets Don Carlos

The Comanche chief bent to the tracks he had just discovered. They were fresh and appeared to be moccasins, not boots.

Quanah knew that another was after Charlie Bird, and these were not those man's tracks. That man wore leather boots with a cross carved into the heel.

He'd seen this "cowboy," or whatever he was, chasing his tail out here on the high plains and had actually fallen into talk with him at a stream crossing. He'd presented himself to the stranger as a well-meaning but hopelessly alcohol-addicted Indian who was after some of the white man's firewater.

"Have you whiskey?" he'd said, holding out his water skin to the man.

"No, son," came the reply. "I haven't tasted the stuff myself in weeks."

The big Indian staggered back a bit and seemed to consider whether to continue the conversation or be on his way. After some thought, he chose to make a bit more conversation with the traveler.

"What bring white man here?" he said, his arms making a sweeping gesture toward the towering cliffs.

"I'm looking for someone. A woman," came the reply. His handsome countenance seemed to light up with an idea. Maybe he could use this savage to find his quarry. He stroked his black mustache as he continued.

"Say, Mr. Indian Chief, have you seen any young white women out this way?"

"No..." was his reply, but something about the way he said it made the other man press the issue further.

"Now then, uh, my good man, maybe I *can* find some firewater around if you can help me find what *I'm* after."

"You say... *hiccup*... you after a white woman? Maybe woman very pretty?"

"Yes!" he exclaimed "Yes! Have you seen them? Tell me, you big lummox, where?"

"Lady wearing hat. Have long black hair?"

"Yes! Yes, that's her! Where is she?"

"Hmmmm... haven't seen them," the native said with a silly grin, and then burst out laughing.

If it was true that Charlie had stolen a white woman, as the rumors on the plains went, then this was probably the right track, Quanah thought. His only hope was that he would reach Charlie before any of the others on his trail, and perhaps save him.

Don Carlos was getting tired of playing games with the drunken tribesman, realizing that he certainly wouldn't be of any assistance in his quest.

"Oh, go on you sot! Get!" he said, looking down at his gun for a split second.

When he raised his head, the Indian was gone. He looked around, expecting to see the man tottering off, but it was as if he had vanished into thin air. Don Carlos slowly turned back to his meal, looking up now and again to check his surroundings with a bit of trepidation.

Gathering Clouds

The United States Army joined the pursuit of Charlie Bird shortly thereafter. Jackson, Don Carlos's trail hand, had made it back after all. He told anyone who would listen about the atrocities committed by the Comanche group that fateful evening. Mackenzie had become interested in finding this rogue and his band, thus ending the reign of terror in his district. He'd also have a chance to exact some personal revenge on Charlie Bird. The new injury smarted almost as much as the wound to his pride that had followed the incident a month ago at the riverbed.

Dust clouds could be seen for miles as the Fourth Cavalry set out from their fort. Across the great plains, the thunder of hundreds of horses' hooves caused the dry earth to quake. Small creatures scurried across the path of the advancing host, scrambling for their burrows.

The inhabitants of the nearby reservation gathered at the gates to watch the procession. They were aware that this could not bode well for their kinfolk who were still out on the plain. Cannons rolled past, pulled by straining steeds, and muscular soldiers on athletic war horses cantered by.

The entire train was led by none other than Mackenzie himself. Perched atop his black horse, three fingers gripping the reins, his posture ramrod straight, he embodied grim determination. Vengeance seethed in his blood and he swore silently to make the one who had caused his latest injury pay dearly.

The people of the plains murmured and wondered. What had caused the white man's army to bare its teeth thus?

A Whole Heap of Trouble

The empty grasses shook with the morning breeze. Charlie Bird inhaled deeply and took in the scents of the high plains. A heady mix of vegetation and wildflowers assaulted his senses.

He stood at the stream and wondered at the swirling eddies and rivulets that formed and disappeared with the flow. If only life's problems would fade as quickly.

Thoughts of past days crept into his consciousness, causing him to no longer hold onto the desire to suppress his emotions.

Little Wing, although dead nearly a year, still loomed large in his mind. He saw her everywhere and in everything. The beauty of a new morning was the most difficult. The very earth seemed to sigh with her breath. She was gone, and his heart ached because of it.

Up to this point, Charlie had been sure there would never be a replacement for his princess, but that had all changed when his band had assaulted the wagon train. This woman—this Rebecca—when she looked at him, sparked feelings he had done everything to kill. Now, those long-forgotten emotions were tearing his soul apart.

He bent his head back and let go with a primal scream. There was nothing else he could do.

The members of the rogue band glanced up from their work with interest. Charlie's scream reverberated off the cliff walls before petering out somewhere over their heads.

Had he met his fate like so many of his brothers before him? A violent death awaited most of the warriors and each knew in his heart that it was only a matter of time. Now it seemed to them that instant had come.

Pahayoko cast his eyes toward the female, the prisoner who had been taken against his will. This trouble had been brought by her. They were hunted now because of that woman. Had he been allowed to dispense with her back at the wagon train, they would still be free to commit their revenge attacks against the white man. Kill her, he reasoned, and there would be a new order. He would be their new leader.

Now, as of the last time they had met with hunters who had given them news, the whole damn US Army was after them. They had stirred up a hornet's nest by capturing a government representative. Killing the other one had not helped matters. Yet this was not the worst news. The worst was that another killer was on their trail. This one was of such fearsome reputation that the mere mention of his name was enough to make one run to the mountains west.

If Charlie were dead, well then that would mean something entirely different. They'd present his body to the authorities and be unimpeded in their quest to exact vengeance on the invaders.

This ironic train of thought was interrupted by Charlie Bird, who burst through the brush.

"Charlie Bird!" Big Bear exclaimed, as they all looked up to see their leader approach the camp. "We had thought you went to join your ancestors!"

"No."

"Have you killed someone then? What made you scream?"

"The trouble we have brought from our last raid bothers my soul."

The man smiled back with Native American humor playing in his eyes. "It troubles us all, brother, but you do not hear us yelling like a buffalo has stuck its horn in our hind quarters."

Charlie could not help but smile back. "Well, we must move

on quickly."

The other man's voice sunk to a whisper. "Charlie, I know the trouble is about her," he said, jerking his hand at the woman who sat cleaning a cloth at the riverside some meters away. "We cannot have her with us! She brings problems and enemies! Why do we have her? We should have taken her scalp or left her at the camp. I know she is of your old people, the Jews, but we are your people now and you must do what is best for the band!"

His voice had slowly risen during his speech, so the other members of the group had noticed the conversation and walked over.

"We must leave her or the white man will not stop until we are all dead!" interjected Pahayoko.

"Yes, we will be destroyed and our revenge on the invaders will never be finished! We can fight small groups, but the whole army can never be defeated by us!" Big Bear declared with feeling.

No one wanted to discuss the real question that hung like knives over all of their heads. Yet after a few moments of the warriors looking at the knives they held in their hands, one of them finally broached the subject.

"What of Quanah? He is after us too! He will get us all!" Pahayoko pounded his fist on his thigh as he spoke.

"Yes," another chimed in with a quivering voice. "I would rather spend many days in a white man's prison than be roasted slowly by Quanah Parker."

"He will make each of us scream!"

Charlie stopped the talk with a gesture. "He will not capture us, the army will not find us, and we will live free on these grasslands forever. Listen brothers, to my plan!"

Plans and Demands Unanswered

Rebecca cast her eyes toward the warriors huddled in conversation. Every now and then one of the men would glance her way and the others would join him. The conversation, held in the Native language unfamiliar to her, was both whispered and shouted as disagreements emerged and were solved. Finally, it appeared as if Charlie had won over the men and they nodded in agreement.

This man, this savage warrior, was actually a civil human with roots back East like her own family. There was more. He was, like her, a Jew. The Lord *did* work in mysterious ways.

One night, a few days earlier, she sat in silence by the fire. All the warriors had lain down for the night and Charlie was sitting up for the first watch. He rested his chin on his hands, elbows planted on his knees as he stared at the flames, which sent their sparks skyward.

She gathered her courage and asked the first question that came to her mind, "Charlie, where are you from?"

"New York," came the response.

"I am from Philadelphia. Back east too."

"Hmph," was all he managed to respond.

"How did you come to be a warrior leader?"

"Long story."

"I think you could elaborate a bit... no one else is here and you've got nothing else to speak about."

"Elaborate? I have not heard that word for many years. OK. If you insist. I will tell you my story."

She chuckled lightly. "Yes, I insist."

A smile curled the edges of his mouth as he continued, "My family came here to this country to make life better for all of us. It was my father who got the notion to open a horse-outfitting store and he brought us west in a wagon. That's when I first caught sight of the plains. I also saw my first Indian and I wished one day I'd ride like them. I guess G-d heard my thoughts, although I'm not sure I would have wanted it to happen the way it did. I still hear my mother's screams when I fall asleep. One day, perhaps, I will tell you."

That was where he left it for the time being. The mystery behind his words was attractive to her, but she couldn't say why.

Closing In

Mackenzie shielded his eyes as he scanned the Llano Estacado for signs of movement. A whip-poor-will fluttered skyward but aside from that the high plains were still, deathly still. The sun was at its peak and the heat was oppressive, and the general wiped his brow with his bad hand. Before dropping his arm, he contemplated the three fingers for a moment. Was it all worth it?

No time for sentimentality. His old wounds ached terribly and he had a rogue to catch. Every moment was precious as he attempted to prevent Charlie from escaping into the distant mountains, where he could spend years hiding without being brought to bay.

He walked purposefully back to his waiting aides and gave the order to move west with extreme haste. The goal was the main thoroughfare that ran east and west across the Staked Plains. He would come from the north and his other wing from the south.

He hoped that Lieutenant Dan had found a path around the edges of the cliffs so as to surround the quarry without alerting them to his presence. A dual pincer movement was the surest way to capture a swift, although outnumbered foe. Mackenzie had used this technique with much success several times before.

Dan had indeed found his way. His two hundred infantry and cavalry wound their way up the cliff face and onto the table of grassland as he watched from horseback. Once assembled, the force would cross the plains single-file until the prey was sighted, then fan out to prevent their escape as Mackenzie closed in from the rear with overwhelming numbers. The ten or so warriors would be killed outright if they didn't surrender, and the girl would hopefully fall into the army's hands.

Dan smiled to himself. If she didn't make it out of the battle, oh well... at least there would be ten less savages and one less Indian sympathizer as a bonus.

Quanah was in deep meditation by the side of one of the many streams that crisscrossed the high plains. He had prayed and thought and prayed some more in hopes of finding and perhaps saving his adopted brother Charlie, who with all of his innate qualities and fighting abilities had gotten himself in over his head. In his quest to somehow assuage the pain of Little Wing's loss, he had brought more trouble down on his own people and made the plains too hot to handle him.

As the Comanche chief stared into the bubbling waters, a plan began to form; ideas took shape and became a scheme. It just might work. It was complicated and involved many things to fall into place but it was worth doing. The more Quanah thought about it, the more he liked the idea. He needed one more actor in the great play he was arranging. He wasn't worried about that.

It would take a tremendous amount of skill for Quanah to find a way to placate the Americans and save his little brother in the process. Luckily for Charlie, skill was what his older brother had in abundance.

Stepping from the quiet of his brushy hideout into the midday sun, Don Carlos waved as the troop of soldiers rode past on their mounts. This was trouble. If those troops got there first and saved the maiden, well, he didn't want to think about that possibility.

He needed some assistance if he was going to succeed in finding her first. Time to find that drunken Indian and enlist his help.

Charlie had just left Rebecca sitting by the creek side when he noted that feeling again. It crept into his consciousness like a pleasant white haze and remained there growing until it was all he could focus on. He wasn't sure what it was about her. She was, if anything, a bit arrogant and plain nasty when she spoke to him. Perhaps it was that energy and self-respect he found enchanting. Charlie was good at many things but understanding his emotions was not one of them.

Now to the plan and its preparation. They would save themselves and perhaps make it better for his Comanche brothers and sisters still on the plains. That Mackenzie and his bloodthirsty Lieutenant Dan had to go and this plan, if it succeeded, would go a long way toward removing the scourge from the Llano Estacado.

He walked to the nearest tree and withdrew his knife from his belt, contemplating before making the mark. This would be the first act in a long chain that would lead to freedom. He pressed the handle of the knife and the deed was done.

Charlie held the knife there for a moment before returning it to its sheath. His mind wandered over the plains and back in time to another turning point in his tumultuous life.

The Guide Partners Up

Don Carlos splashed the water from the pond on his face. The cool liquid felt good as it cascaded down his moustache. He was, if nothing else, careful about personal grooming. It was one those things he needed for his own benefit, not so much for others; although the looks he often received from ladies young and old alike told him his efforts were not wasted on those of the fairer sex.

After the ripples settled, he pulled his Bowie knife from its scabbard and began to shave his face in the reflection of the still water. As he lifted the blade to his face, a savage visage appeared over his shoulder.

Startled, he rolled away and looked into the countenance of the big, dumb Indian he'd met earlier.

"Now, what the hell is wrong with you!" he demanded. "You better be careful that you don't sneak up on people like that! Nearly scared the wits out o' me!"

The savage just stared back with a silly grin plastered across his face.

"Well, what do you want?"

"What you think, white man?" came the reply.

"Whiskey, huh? Didn't I tell you last time I didn't have any for you? You must be either desperate or stupid or both! Now go on! Get out of here!" and Don Carlos reached for his pistol.

"I don't hurt you! No gun! See?" and he held his large palms out for the guide to see.

The hand eased away from the pistol but stayed at the ready just in case.

The Native kept the grin. "I can help you, Mister, I know how to find the girl you look for!"

"How do you know what I'm after? You following me? I should shoot you!" The wicked-looking Navy Colt revolver flashed in the morning sun as Don Carlos withdrew it from its holster.

The Indian's hands shot up as his smile changed to a look of alarm. "You don't shoot! I don't follow you! I know from the army men. I sometimes help them too! They pay with whiskey and I track for them. This time they tell me about girl from East captured by Comanches. I guess you look for her too."

Now the white man relaxed in his manner and lowered his gun.

"OK, so you'll help me find her?"

The big native nodded emphatically. "I know where the Comanche group hide!"

"OK then, I suppose you want some whiskey for your troubles?"

Again, he nodded.

"OK, we have a deal. I hope you're a good tracker."

"Best!"

Don Carlos procured his hand. "Don Carlos is my name."

The Indian jovially grasped the hand and said, "Quanah Parker is my name!"

The Way Things Turned Out

Charlie gazed from afar at Rebecca. His father would be proud of him, Charlie thought. He was strong, self-sufficient, and a leader of men. But certain things, Charlie knew would bother his father. Charlie was, after all, a warrior—which meant killing, something he knew his father found abhorrent.

Additionally, being a Comanche meant raiding, and raiding meant scalping, stealing, and many other manners of mayhem—all perpetrated in order to cow the enemy into submission. The one last thing Charlie knew would be a thorn in his father's side—had he known about it—was his marriage to a Native maiden. As early as he could remember, his father had been very clear on that one point. He must wed someone from his people: the Jewish nation.

"Charlie," Mr. Heintzelman had intoned seriously one night, shortly before the capture of his son. "You must be sure to remain a Jew. Our people have died and been thrown from nearly every nation on this earth, and we have remained a nation regardless. This is unprecedented in history, and we must—you must—continue in this tradition. Please, when the times comes…" he said, grabbing Charlie's shoulders in a firm but loving grip. He then looked directly into his son's watery blue eyes and added, "You must marry a girl who is Jewish! Promise me that!"

"I promise, Papa!" is what Charlie had said.

It hadn't seemed like such a difficult request at the time, nor too relevant. He had only been nine years old, after all. Little had he known that this would be a test he would find difficult to pass some ten and two years later while out on the high plains of the Llano Estacado. Yet perhaps, here, seated a few feet away was the answer to his father's unspoken prayers. Might as well talk to her some more.

He was coming her way! She did her best to straighten her ruffled dress.

"We will be heading out soon. Please prepare yourself for a long trip."

"I would like to know to where we're headed, my good sir."

Charlie liked her pluck. Most captives shuddered and turned inward. She had, after discovering he spoke English, never taken his word for anything—but always questioned it.

"I will let you know all that you have to know. For now, you have to trust me."

"How can I? Who knows what you have in store? You are more savage than any other white man!"

At these last words, he became enraged. His fists clenched and his brow felt hot, yet he controlled himself.

"How could you possibly say that?" he asked, his calm voice hiding the anger and frustration within. "I have done what I could for you. The only reason you are not dead and left to rot is because of my intervention."

"Have I offended you?" She spoke demurely, "I didn't mean to, but I am here," and her voice rose in volume a bit, "because your band attacked our caravan. And what's worse is that instead of sending me back to my people, you take me out here in the middle of nowhere; and now you expect me to trust you?" She folded her arms and waited for him to answer.

He gathered his thoughts for a moment as his brow clouded.

"You have no choice, Rebecca!" he growled. And with that, he turned on his heel and headed back toward the war party.

The Swirl of Life

Rebecca was running after Charlie. That last little bit had been too much and her protector seemed genuinely insulted. That had not been her intent.

"Charlie!" she called out. "I didn't mean to hurt your feelings! I just wanted to know what's happening with me. I think I have a right to know," she gasped as she caught up.

Charlie turned, smiling, arms folded.

"I didn't know you cared about my feelings."

"I... I don't like to hurt anyone's feelings," she stammered and a blush crept to her cheeks. "I just think I should know what you're planning on doing! It's my safety!"

"You have to trust me. I know what I'm doing. I will get you out of this and save my friends here too."

Just then Big Bear ran over and began speaking in his native dialect.

"Charlie Bird! I heard yelling and I thought maybe she was beating you!" the man joked.

Switching seamlessly back to the Comanche language, Charlie laughed, "No but she almost did! We have work to do and I need her to cooperate. I was just convincing her!"

"Ha! OK, I understand!" He winked at Charlie Bird and bowed comically to the girl, then walked off to join the rest of the group.

"What did you say?" she demanded, again assuming a guarded position.

"Just that I need your cooperation and that you agreed to do what you are supposed to do."

"I did no such thing!"

"Well, let's put it this way. If you don't, none of us will make it out of here!"

"I have no choice then?"

"No, you don't." And with a hand to his brow, he bowed in mock civility and joined his compatriots, leaving a frowning Rebecca to her thoughts.

As the water ebbed and flowed against the creek bank, Rebecca wondered to herself at the waters of life. The river swirled about in seemingly random directions but always somehow ended up in the same place. Life was like that, she mused. Regardless of the twists and turns of it, all people ended in the same spot. Some by more circuitous routes to be sure.

How had she, an Eastern woman of Victorian manners and progressive thought, come to be a captive of a savage band on the staked plains of the vast American West?

"Not where you thought you would be at this point, eh?" Charlie seemed to break in on her thoughts.

He had seemingly appeared from nowhere and Rebecca, briefly startled, looked up with something akin to annoyance on her face. Somehow she could not bring herself to be angry with this boyish warrior. He had saved her, but her feelings went beyond gratitude. His charm, to her, ran deeper than his good looks and athletic carriage could explain.

The young brave sat down on the rock next to her and crossed his legs, giving her a crooked smile. She felt her cheeks warm.

"Do you think I imagined being here 12 years ago in New York?" he began. "I lived in a filthy walk-up tenement on Avenue A with my family stuffed into one room. My mother, educated as she was, cleaned rich people's mansions on 5th Avenue. My father bounced from job to job. Then, one day my parents heard of an opportunity for land out in Texas and we started out for a new life. A new life! Ha!"

"What happened then, Charlie?"

"What happened? Within a year my father was dead and I was the man of the house. Next thing I knew, I was doing all of the work around and had to leave school. One day, I was tending to the family horses when they came out of the forest."

"Who did?"

"The Comanche. They had been raiding a nearby village and had heard of the beautiful horses we kept. I tried to run but they were on their mounts and I was on foot. The old man who took it upon himself to protect us after father died dropped a few of them but could not prevent them from throwing me over the saddle of a horse and taking me back to their camp."

"Did you try to run away? I would have!"

"That's not in my nature. As you may have guessed already, I don't flee from trouble when I think I'm cornered. I fight back!" he said with some feeling as he clenched his fists tightly.

Rebecca did not know if it was wise to prod him into telling the rest of his story but her curiosity got the best of her, as it usually did.

"What did you do when they brought you to their camp?"

Charlie looked away for a moment before turning to her again and answered with a smile. "I fought with everything I had. Oh, it was not a battle I could win, but I was so mad that they had taken me from my mother and siblings that I was nearly blind with rage. I was nearly killed by the tribe as I ranted and raved. I struck an older boy and he nearly beat me into the next world. It was only the chief, who saw my fighting spirit who stopped him. Only when the leader made promises to protect my family did I agree to join the Comanche and become one of them."

"That is quite a story! Who was the boy who almost killed you?"

Charlie grinned as one who is friends with important people sometimes will.

"Have you never heard of Quanah Parker?"

Charlie's Story

April 1859, New York City

The Heintzelman family had never really found their footing in the new world. Mr. Joseph Heintzelman had been through a slew of employments, from tailoring to a stint as a yeoman on the New York docks. He had attempted every vocation with little success.

After being told not to return next Monday for the tenth time, he returned to the East Village tenement his family shared with several other recent immigrants. Making his way past the slums on Avenue A, he wished for some way to provide security for his growing family.

He struck the stone curb in frustration, and a piece of stone bounced into the street. Joseph looked up from his reverie and watched the stone tumble, feeling much the same as it looked—dislodged from his familiar surroundings and cast about in a sea of uncertainty. A horse and carriage trundled by, the smell of the horses drifting forth into the stagnant July air. From the carriage dropped a white sheet of paper. On that paper was writing. German writing.

Joseph stepped into the street to pick it up and shook it clean. It was an announcement in German about a land grant. This was something he could understand. With a new sense of hope, he breathed in the fresh air of the humid New York summer.

The words on the sign spoke to him. They promised a new future somewhere out west. Free loans, land, and freedom! This was the American dream he had worked so hard for, the one for which he had departed his old land. He would go home and tell his wife, and they would start packing tonight!

Joseph Heintzelman burst through the door of his second-floor walk-up apartment with an energy he had not demonstrated in years. His wife, who had been doing something with the laundry, was startled and formed an unspoken question with her lips.

Responding to her look, Joseph raised his voice in his excitement. "Rachel! We are going west! Now, gather the kids and we'll leave this dirty life behind us!" As he spoke, he gestured expansively, pointing in a direction he supposed was west.

"Wait… where?" Rachel stammered.

"West, my girl! West!" He had called her by a name he hadn't used in a very long time, not since they had lived in Germany over ten years before.

"What will we do there? How will we survive?"

"We'll open a horse-outfitting store like my family had in the old country! This flyer says they give loans for free to those who want to open a business! There's plenty of people and space aplenty, and they give land for free! We can build a home with room for all! No more living like rats with rotten walls!" And with that, he struck the old, gray wall with the side of his fist, causing pieces of debris to tumble to the floor in a small cloud.

Mrs. Heintzelman was warming to the idea already, beginning to dream the dreams she had suppressed for some time. After crossing the seas to America, she had come to accept her lot as that of a lower-class worker's wife. She couldn't shop in the fancy stores that were springing up north of Washington Square park like glimmering jewels. The well-heeled women whose families had established themselves as bankers and businessmen years before tossed their money about like it was mere paper, buying the most expensive dresses and furs without thinking twice. Rachel was lucky to buy a pair of shoes once a year for the High Holidays.

She worked for one of these uptown women as a cleaner on the weekends. She hated toiling on Saturdays, as she had been raised as a Jew in Germany and had always kept the Sabbath day holy before arriving on the shores of the United States. Here, it was just not possible to abstain from working as Saturday was a regular day for the laboring class. It was a good thing in a way, since her husband had not been that religious at home. He was more for the new ideas of equality and thought all people, gentile or Jew, were alike. On such a topic, they differed, and Rachel suffered alone in that respect.

The jealousy hurt too. She had never been rich in her home country, but she had been comfortable, comfortable enough to buy herself and her children nice things to eat and fancy things to wear. The woman she now worked for would have thought nothing of burning hundred-dollar bills to keep warm, while Rachel was lucky just to have enough black bread and potatoes to keep herself and her growing family from starving. That was difficult enough, since her husband was constantly being tossed from one job to the next— therefore, never really earning much. She often cursed the day she had agreed to travel to these shores!

The new opportunity grew like a sunburst in her mind until it took on a life of its own. Suddenly, a thought crept into her mind and cast a cloud on the bright, new future.

"But Joseph, what of the other people there? Are there any Jewish people? Will we be the only ones? We must have a community!"

"Ah! That is perhaps the best part of the whole thing! There are others of our people that are already there and prospering! There are more among the group we will join that are Hebrews as well!"

That sealed it for her, and she caught the excitement and carried it a step further by yanking the family's trunk from behind the old stove and throwing it open.

"Let's pack, Joseph!"

Joseph then stepped across the room and embraced his wife, feeling years younger and ready for anything.

Somewhere near San Antonio, Texas, September 1859

As the wagons that held the Heintzelman family and all their worldly possessions neared the famous Texas frontier town of San Antonio, a nine-year-old Charlie pulled back the flaps of canvas that had been shielding the three boys within from the piercing late-summer sun. He had never seen anything quite like the vistas that now presented themselves to his young eyes.

Vast stretches of undulating plains spanned for miles in every direction. The flora that grew in this part of the country was as alien to a New Yorker as a Chinese vase would have been to an African Bushman in the jungles of the Congo. Stunted trees spread their thick branches wide among the barrel-shaped cacti. The landscape was comprised of mostly brown and sandy tones, broken every so often by a bright, vibrant flower.

The barren land held hidden riches for those who knew how to coax nutrients from the soil. In a few years, those resources would be insignificant in comparison to the huge black gold reserves that resided a few meters below the surface. Oil barons would soon make their Eastern counterparts look positively penniless with the wealth they would draw from the Texas dirt.

Sammy, Charlie's youngest brother, whined plaintively from the back of the wagon, "Mommy! When will we be there?"

His mother leaned in from the front of the wagon, her soft voice calming his impatience. "Dear, a little bit longer and we'll be at our new home. Your father says it's only a day or two from San Antonio!"

"But Mommy, we have been traveling for so, so long. I've already forgotten what New York looks like!"

Charlie rolled his eyes as he continued to scan his surroundings. Little brothers could be oh so bothersome! As for himself, he couldn't wait to get to their new homestead and explore. It would surely be more exciting and free than the old tenement back in New York. He could barely contain his excitement as he took in every sight, sound, and smell.

Turning his attention to the west, he witnessed yet another incredible occurrence. It seemed at first as if the horizon had become misty. Slowly, this mist crystallized into a dust cloud that grew as whatever was causing it approached. A faint rumble, which could at first be felt more than heard, became a roar as a great mass of beasts materialized like some massive ship emerging from a fog. There were perhaps one hundred thousand animals in the herd, and the earth quaked as they drew nearer to the travelers.

Charlie's father, Joseph, steered the wagon toward a small hillock jutting from the plains. The tide of animals was headed their way and he wanted to be on safer ground. As the buffalo thundered towards them, the noise became deafening. Everything shook with the force of an earthquake as the herd swept around the elevation in a raging torrent of fur and hooves.

Mrs. Heintzelman climbed into the wagon to be with her younger children as Charlie joined his father on the front seat. It was all they could do to keep their balance with the ground vibrating beneath them. Charlie had the same feeling whenever a thunderstorm threatened—excitement coupled with fascination.

Suddenly, an even more interesting thing happened that locked Charlie's attention in yet another direction. From behind a towering butte sped an Indian on horseback. He wound his way toward the herd like a wraith until he spotted the leading animal. Pulling his arm back in a practiced motion, he hurled a short, feathered, deadly-looking spear at the animal.

The beast, thus struck between the ribs, gave a roar and stumbled headfirst into the ground. After a few heaves and twitches, it lay still. Then, a great commotion ensued as the entire herd came to an abrupt halt; it was as if they didn't know how to continue once the front-running buffalo had been killed.

The Indian called out in his own language and several others from his tribe joined him on horseback. They quickly descended on the dead animal, chopping its two-thousand-pound bulk into more manageable pieces with their knives.

Each of the party then slung a portion of the animal across their light horses and rode off in a file. The rest of the buffalo milled about for a time and then, choosing a new leader, followed him in a great mass toward the horizon.

The Heintzelman family watched all of this, mouths agape, from the safety of their wagon atop the knoll. Each had a different impression and took away something unique. There was one, the nine-year-old boy, who wished that he could be one of the Indians, riding free across the neverending Texas landscape and performing feats of incredible prowess from horseback.

Little did he know what the future held for himself and for his family.

Kerrville, Texas, October 1859

Joseph Heintzelman stopped his wagon just short of Kerrville's main street along the Guadalupe River, which split the town in twain. As the water gurgled along toward its destination farther east, so too the people of this bustling frontier town traveled in the directions of their current occupations.

The dusty streets were full of residents on their way to or from work of some sort. Whether it was the new mill being constructed along the bluff above the town, or the shingle shop that had been the original economic raison d'etre of the village, the bustle of industry was everywhere.

The head of the Heintzelman household liked what he saw. Here was a place he could set up shop, and his hard work would be rewarded with accomplishment, both monetary and spiritual.

The rest of the clan shared his sentiment. Mrs. Heintzelman squeezed her husband's arm with excitement as she peered around, eyes wide.

"Joseph," she spoke gleefully. "This place is our new home! Can you feel it too?"

Her husband nodded his concurrence as his gaze swiveled in all directions.

"Papa!" came a call from the back of the wagon. "Is this the place?"

"Yes, it is, Chaim!" Joseph leaned toward his son as he spoke. "What do you think?"

Chaim, or Charlie as the rest of his family called him, was a precocious nine years old and the eldest of the children. He was also intelligent beyond his years. Brushing the hair from his eyes, he joined his parents on the wagon seat.

"It is wonderful, Papa!"

There was some sort of feeling—excitement combined with hope—that seemed contagious. The rest of the children made their way to the front and stood behind their parents and eldest sibling. They basked in the good feeling as their father checked the slip of paper that contained the address at which they would be staying.

"It's this way, I believe," the patriarch announced as he prodded his horses forward with a cluck of his tongue and a gentle application of the whip.

As the family pulled up in front of what was to be their home, the man who had been sitting on the front step raised his hat to see who was sitting in the wagon.

"Ho there, friend!" the man called from his seat. "You must be Joseph Heintzelman, or I'm much mistaken." He got up and strode across the dirt lawn. Joseph climbed down from his wagon and gripped the man's proffered hand.

"Nice to meet you, I'm sure. You must be Mr. Kalrmenster."

"Indeed I am. We're excited to have a northern businessman here to show us how a horse outfitting store is run!" he exclaimed while smiling broadly.

"And I am excited to do so! Is this the house?" he asked, pointing his riding whip at the small but neat structure.

"Exactly. As I said in my last letter, it's no mansion, but I think you and your family will find it comfortable."

"Well children, let's get our stuff and get settled in!"

Kerrville, Texas, December 1859

A light snow began to fall as Mrs. Heintzelman called her children in from their outdoor chores. As they came in and shook off the cold, one did not appear.

Wrapping her shawl about her shoulders, Rachel walked out into the cold afternoon. The wind cut into her with icy fingers, so she wrapped herself more tightly. As she stepped atop the hill, she scanned the horizon.

Where was that boy? Charlie was her eldest and just loved to explore. He often wandered far from home amongst the crags and forests of the Texas hill country. After returning some evenings, he would recount his adventures to his younger siblings as they sat awestruck by the fire.

Rachel would sit in the corner, finishing her sewing as she listened to her son spin yarns for the brood. She worried about his antics at times, but she always smiled inwardly and perhaps even envied his free spirit. When Charlie slept, she could make out his father in his young features. His mere presence was all the more precious after the passing of Mr. Heintzelman earlier in the year.

Now that the stories of Indian atrocities had been circulating, she worried more than was perhaps warranted. The tensions had been building, especially along the southern borders of the Comanche range.

There hadn't been an attack in Kernstown in recent memory and the Indians seemed to stay far from there. There was, after all, no buffalo hunting or infringement on their territory committed by the well-meaning residents of the hamlet. The politics of survival never stopped the Indian population from making war on their white neighbors if that was what was called for. A push from ranchers and their cattle to consume the grass stretching across the high plains was inflaming the situation, and the war path had brought native raiders to the area.

Something made her turn. She couldn't tell if it was a noise, a feeling, or what. Her gaze followed the tree line, which was already cloaked in a shroud of snow, its stark white coating cast upon a dark green wall.

What was that speck at the edge of the field near the forest? She could see the spot growing larger as it ran at top speed across the fields toward the house. It was soon followed by several other marks, larger and approaching the former at great speed. As the shapes drew nearer, they morphed into a runner fleeing for his life from the gathering menace of horsed Indians.

Her gaze fell on that running form. She could now make out Charlie waving his hands and screaming to get inside and shut the door! Mrs. Heintzelman froze, not knowing whether to run toward her son or run inside and protect the rest of her family as best she could.

The decision was made for her by a shot that echoed off the hills from behind her. The closest native fell from his horse with a groan and was trodden under foot by his mount. He lay still after the dust had settled, lifeless and defeated.

Rachel whirled to see where the shot had come from and noticed Old Man Gerber, the same who had welcomed them upon their arrival, standing tall with his Colt repeating rifle raised to his shoulder. Smoke billowed from the barrel.

A second large-caliber bullet rocketed forth and another Indian saddle was emptied. It appeared that the boy might actually escape as most of the pack of braves reigned up and jumped off their horses, hiding behind them as shields. There was one displaying incredible horsemanship, however, who managed to slip to the side of his steed and within an eyeblink had scooped the youth up and thrown him over the back of his horse.

A mother screamed, an old man fired his gun, and a kicking, thrashing boy was carried off into the woods by a savage warrior who was soon joined by the rest of the raiding party.

Later That Day

The boy was thrown unceremoniously from the horse. Landing on his shoulder, the youngster sprang to his feet, fists clenched and ready for action.

"Come on!" he screamed. "I will fight all of you!"

Crouched in fighting position, Charlie turned in place, attempting to face all of his captors at once.

A smiling Indian warrior merely shook his head and descended from his horse, carrying a long and vicious-looking knife. He strode over toward the youth and grabbed his hair roughly, bending the child's head back and exposing the neck.

Charlie's eyes grew wide but he did not cry or plead for his life; instead he gazed furiously into the eyes of his tormentor.

Shrugging, the big native raised his knife to finish the job when an authoritative voice rose from inside the nearest teepee.

"Stop!" the chief called in his native tongue as he stepped

majestically from a flap in the side of the tent. "This young one has the tough spirit and we need more hunters for the buffalo and warriors for our protection!"

The big Indian that was holding the boy released his grip and shoved him toward the tribal head.

The chief spoke in stilted yet clear English.

"What is your name, boy?"

The man, whose only sign of leadership was a woven blanket and single eagle feather worn in his hair, bent low to speak with the boy at his height. The tribe was in desperate need of hunters and warriors. Smallpox had ravaged the Comanche ranks and the sparse, protein-rich diet of the plains had caused infertility. To survive, they needed to increase their population through capture.

"I shall not tell you! Return me to my family!"

The head looked up at his warriors with a grin and nodded as if in confirmation of his original assessment.

He straightened and extended a hand, smiling.

"My name is Nacona! I welcome you!"

"Welcome me? To what?"

"To your new home with our family!" the chief spoke while gesturing with a sweeping motion.

"I only wish to return to my family! You people have stolen my mother's oldest son and my father is dead!"

The chief spared no words; just like the pulling of a tooth, he felt it better to get it over with quickly.

"You will never go back! That is your old life. Your new life is here with us on the plains, hunting the buffalo!"

As these words and the enormity of their import sunk in, a sudden feeling of dizziness overtook the lad and he fell to his knees. Then he vomited.

When he was finished retching, he looked up at the surrounding warriors, who had remained silent and respectful during his moment of physical weakness. He searched their faces and when he found that of the chief, he stood to his full height, puffed up his chest, and stated in as dignified a manner as possible, "I will never become part of your tribe if my my mother and brothers and sisters are to starve because I am not there to provide for them! They shall want for protection and shelter without me!"

This devotion to his family did not go unnoticed by the Comanche leader and he placed a fatherly hand on the youth's shoulder.

"If I promise you that they will never go hungry and they shall never be bothered," he began with feeling, thinking of his own mother, "will you then promise that you will never go back to them?"

"If I refuse?"

"Then we cannot guarantee their safety or yours!"

Charlie gritted his teeth, balled his fists and looked up at the leader through his matted hair.

"I agree, but," he stated with barely contained fury, his finger pointed menacingly at the chief's chest, "if you do not keep your promise, I shall kill you with my own bare hands!"

Nacona frowned, extended a muscled brown hand to the boy, and said simply, "Deal!"

Charlie reached out as well and with that grasp, wedded his future to that of this nomadic and noble tribe.

Rebecca's Story

Looking up and grinning Charlie said, "And now, dear Rebecca, I've told you my story. You owe me the pleasure of hearing your story!"

She blushed at being addressed in such a fashion, but she did not feel the usual revulsion when a man turned his attentions towards her.

"Sure. I'll tell you but please be patient because I've got to start my tale a long time ago..."

Being of the aristocracy was not the only way to get ahead in the small world that was the Jewish community of Philadelphia during the years preceding the war. One could be a member of the Rabbinate, a politician or a merchant who struck it rich. The Katz family would one day achieve the coveted status of "a noted family" in the latter category.

They were a simple lot, hardworking and pious, having come over in the early 50's from Germany to better themselves. Herman was the patriarch and he had established a small trading route which sent him for months on end out along the country roads with his wagon selling wares to the small farmers and workers of Pennsylvania and Western Maryland.

Initially he pushed his own cart over hills and down into green valleys. At some point he had enough to buy a mule of his own and things got a bit easier. There were times in those early days that he would sit by a lonely campfire and dream of being reunited with his beloved wife and infant daughter. Half of everything he made he sent back to Germany for their care. The other half was split many ways. He kept very little for himself.

Herman wore out many a boot sole and horseshoe in his travels before he had collected enough to send for his family. First, his younger brothers, Samuel and Irving, would make the long journey by ship, joining the business and solidifying the concern.

They opened a store on main street in Lower Merion and did steady, if not overly lucrative, business. Herman was always thinking of new ways to make money and more often than not, he succeeded. Samuel and Irving would work the front of the house, making sure customers felt at home, which of course meant they would stay longer in the long aisles and spend more money.

The older brother spent hours upon hours, sleeves rolled up, pouring over his books to see where he profited most. He would then make whatever changes he felt necessary and the business would grow.

Soon, the shop, Katz and Co., took up half a block on the main thoroughfare. The gilt posts leading into the store belied a huge selection of goods. From flour and grains to horse collars and luxurious furniture, the bounty of the industrial revolution and its incredible production capacity could all be found sitting atop their shelves.

Finally, the day came when Herman felt secure enough financially to send for Hannah and his daughter. He waited with bated breath on the New York docks for the ship to make its appearance. Knowing from personal experience how arduous the Atlantic crossing could be in steerage, he had sprung for first class accommodations for his wife and child. They would experience none of the sickening swaying, cramped quarters, and poor quality food of the lower class.

The better traveling arrangements also meant that they would not have to wait with the poor souls at Ellis Island as they were checked for disease and worthiness of entry to the United States. It was an expedited process and not nearly as traumatizing from his own experience as a poor immigrant.

After months of waiting anxiously, there they were! Waving from the railing, he spied his beautiful wife in a neat dress and straw hat. There they were! Waving from the railing he spied the beautiful woman in a neat dress and straw hat. Below her mother, grasping the railings was a wide-eyed girl of seven, taking in the new world.

Precocious and lively, Rebecca, for that was the child's name, grew into the belle of the community and the jewel of her father's heart. Herman worshipped the ground she walked on. When there were days he felt that he couldn't go on, he would think of the girl and his cares would vanish. A very wonderful thing is the love of a father for his daughter.

Things went well for some time and Rebecca grew up in a loving home. She would attend the local synagogue on the Sabbath with her family. Sitting next to her mother, she learned of the great traditions that were the bedrock of the Jewish faith come to life.

The Rabbi would speak of the ancient Hebrews as they left Egypt or discuss their trials and tribulations for the 40 years they were in the desert, seeking a land in which to fulfill G-d's word. He would talk of the Sabbath itself and delve into questions that new discoveries would mean to the observance of the holy day of rest.

Most interesting of all were the discussions of slavery and the "proper Jewish view" regarding that "curious institution." The Bible itself mentioned slavery and even sanctioned it, yet it was not to be carried out in the cruel manner of the Southern plantation owner. The Talmud even stated that if one acquires a slave, he acquires a master.

The Katz' family would have lively discussions about the question of slavery at their Sabbath meal. Rebecca always argued for the emancipation of slaves as she could never reconcile the practice with her views of right and wrong. Her father stated emphatically that, although he abhorred the cruel treatment of slaves, he felt that it was not the place of one man to tell another what to do.

Sometimes these arguments would grow heated and Rebecca's mother would mediate the discussion, kissing both her husband and her daughter on the head, effectively bringing the conflict to a close. They were, above all else, a loving family.

Then, the war came. And so too the crash.

Herman enlisted in the army with the general idea of patriotism coupled with a desire to keep the Union together, despite his opposition to emancipation in general.

He was wounded ever so slightly in the First Battle of Manassas as he charged down the hill in support of Burnside's troops. A ball nicked his hand and he dropped his rifle, which effectively ended the fighting for him that day.

The man wrote to his wife and daughter that day of the fight. He described the great lines of men marching across the fields in the face of the most incredible fire. Shells bursting amongst the men, flinging bodies skyward. Such bravery was never seen on this fine lad, he had declared.

Mrs. Katz read the letter, relieved that her husband had made it through with only a small scratch. She equally heartened by the missive stating that although the North had not been victorious that day, the war would soon be over. The Confederacy had not the staying power to withstand the ever-tightening Union blockade.

Rebecca, reading the same letter, took something entirely different from it. She felt intensely proud that her "Papa" was fighting the good fight to free the country of slavery once and for all. He was on the front lines and doing "good service to G-d and country!" Her father was doing something important and meaningful.

The next year found Herman Katz on the Peninsula with McClellan and his tremendous host pinning General Johnston to his works as the fate of the Confederate capitol, Richmond, hung in the balance.

The great army made a push for the destruction of the Confederacy at a place called Fair Oaks. Johnston fell gravely wounded and would be replaced, fortunately for the South, by the military genius, Robert E. Lee.

At the same battle where the Southern army leaders changed, Herman Katz was shot while rallying his comrades around the company flag. He fell and died amongst the smoke, screams, and fire, his daughter the last thing on his mind before everything faded to black.

Alas, Samuel and Irving were not cut from the same cloth as their brother, Herman. Upon learning of his elder sibling's death, Samuel, blackguard that he turned out to be, fled to Europe with most of the family fortune never to be heard from again. What was left, Irving mismanaged, being somewhat of an imbecile.

Soon enough, the fine showroom closed and Ella Katz and her daughter found themselves destitute and bereft of any means to support themselves. Luckily, they were members of a small but flourishing Jewish community. At the least, they would have food and shelter from their neighbors. Their status was irretrievable however, and a dim future awaited the pair.

After they sold their house to pay off the debts the business had accrued, they moved in with the Salomons, a well-to-do family that had been in the United States for over a century. The quarters were comfortable, but Mrs. Katz would sit up for nights, mourning her husband and bemoaning her fate.

This was too much for the spirited Rebecca to deal with and she told her mother so one night following supper.

"Mother! How can you just sit here and cry! Are you not ashamed of yourself? We must do what we can to better our lot!"

The elder Katz woman turned a tear-stained face to her daughter and her lower lip began to tremble.

Finally, after regarding her child for a moment, she spoke in a choked voice. "How can you talk so, Rebbeca? After all I have been through, you still have no compassion for your poor old mother?"

Rebecca stomped her foot impatiently. "Mother, we have become a charity case! I notice all the people in the streets and how they regard us with pity! Sometimes I cannot hold my head straight for the shame. I will not stand it any longer!"

"But, my dear, what are we to do? All that we have is the clothes on our backs and a few old relics..." she began passionately. "What are a woman and her barely of age daughter to do? Shall we begin again? I cannot! I have not the energy."

Her daughter stopped her mid-sentence. "You have not the will. If you prefer to sulk and keen, then so be it!"

"What will you do? You won't leave your mother alone, will you?" At the idea, Ella broke into a fit of sobs.

Rebecca waited for this latest outburst to play itself out before bending down and holding her mother's face in her hands.

"Mother, I will never leave you! Even if I am away, I will always be in your heart. But I cannot resign myself to a pitiful existence like this. I will hold my head high once again! I am off to New York to teach the Free Negroes."

Her mother could not contain her surprise. "What are you going to do?"

"I am going to teach. To better the world. I have already spoken to the agent, Mr. Williams, and he has secured me a billet. I am leaving in a fortnight!"

Mrs. Katz fell on her face and screamed. "You have done all this behind my back! And now you are leaving me to this miserable fate!"

A tear sprang to Rebecca's eye but her resolve did not weaken.

"I will send you money, all that I can and when I meet the right man, I will marry and send for you!"

"You say that, Rebecca but how will I know? You will be a sheep among wolves!"

"I can take care of myself." She sank to her knees next to her mother and her voice softened, "I will always be careful. And... I shall never forget my promise to come get you when the time is right."

The door opened, a dress ruffled, and Rebecca fled from the room, leaving her mother to wonder what the future held for her daughter and herself.

Those Ain't What You Think They Are!

Lieutenant Dan had seen these tracks before. Just where escaped him at the moment, but he knew there was significance in their presence here on the dry ground.

They stretched into the distance and appeared as if something heavy—some beast or other—had made them. There was a split in each of the tracks and each came to a point like a spade.

Then it came to him, what they were and why it struck him as strange seeing them here. They were obviously from the Buffalo that roamed the plains, yet they were left singly, not in a great multitude as was usually the case. They also seemed to double in a few places and then resume their single-file imprint on the plains.

Dan called to one of his subordinates, "Thompson! Get over here! What do you make of these?" he pointed at the ground as the young sergeant ran over to see what his superior wanted.

"It looks like a Buffalo left these, but it don't seem right," he replied while pushing the blond curls from his face with a dirty hand.

"Yes, I agree. Almost like a person wearing shoes that look like animal feet! And they stagger a bit too. Like someone who has been drinking a bit too much!"

"Yessir! That seems a good probability. What shall we do about it? Not too important, I think."

"It might not be, Thompson. But then again, they may have been fooling us this whole time. They crossed and crisscrossed our paths and we didn't notice because of our looking for the wrong thing!"

"Well... what was it we were looking for?"

"You dunderhead! Can't you see? We've been looking for Indian tracks, but we should have been looking for buffalo tracks!"

Thompson removed his cap and scratched his head with a look of comical thought. "Well, I still don't get why we should have been looking for buffalo when we was tracking Indians!"

Dan was losing patience with his aide's slow uptake on the meaning behind these tracks and he let him have it with both barrels, as it were.

"Get you stupid dumb self back with the troops! I will never understand why Mackenzie promoted an idiot like you!"

As Thompson slank back to his command, Dan set about writing a letter in his tent. Mackenzie would be thrilled to hear that he was onto something and the approval of his superior meant, to him, nearly as much as a promotion.

When he finished writing his letter and had sent it off with a courier, he began to make plans for following these tracks to where they led—to glory, he hoped.

An hour later, the lieutenant stretched his limbs, emitting a satisfied grunt. He watched the sky turn colors with the setting of the sun over the Llano Estacado. He never tired of this view.

He ordered the horses hobbled for the night and turned back to his tent to complete his instructions.

Tomorrow would be a great day!

Quanah and Don Carlos sat concealed about a hundred feet

away. They poked their heads above the rocks and watched their foe retreat inside.

Looking at each other, they couldn't resist their smiles, teeth glinting in the setting sun. It seemed as though their plans were coming together rather well!

Running the Fox to Ground

The thing was set, or so it seemed to Charlie. His plan was coming together and if all went well, he'd be able to slip away from the hornets' nest that had been stirred up. He would save his comrades so they could perhaps find peace and happiness elsewhere as these high plains held nothing for them except pain and the memories of loved ones lost.

There were two conundrums that puzzled him and he, despite all his cunning, was unable to see a way to solve the problems.

The first was the fact he would probably never again be able to see the beloved high plains, waving grass, and steep cliffs that caught the sun just so that they were painted with all the glories of creation. The second was that his plan made no contingency for Rebecca. She would be left to fend for herself once she decided to break away from the group, and she would be allowed to once the final act was set in motion. Charlie wasn't sure he would be able to let her leave so quickly, not that it was his choice.

The way he felt about her was something he had never felt for anyone, even Little Wing. It was a deeper connection, something that transcended mere attraction or even common interests. It was if she had been placed there for him to find in this world. His logic told him that he should not feel this way, since Little Wing had been gone for such a short amount of time, but his heart told him otherwise.

Experience told him the best way to handle insoluble problems was to face them head on. He may find another place on Earth dear to his heart, but never another like Rebecca.

His mind made up, he tied the final bunch of sticks together and sought her out.

Rebecca, the captive teacher, was sitting with her back against a tree writing something when she noticed Charlie emerge from the nearby copse of trees. He was headed in her direction and she blushed despite her best efforts to seem indifferent. This crazy Indian rogue was, in reality, anything but the heartless warrior he liked so much to portray.

MacKenzie crumpled the letter in his good hand and tossed the note into the corner.

"Damn that fool!" he hissed to himself between clenched teeth.

"Sir?" The aid poked his head in.

No reply came as the general brushed past the surprised subordinate.

He flung the tent flap aside and stepped into the blaring sunlight. Shielding his eyes, MacKenzie looked toward the Cap Rock.

Somewhere on that wild plateau of waving grass and vast space, half of his force was being led into a trap by an overzealous lieutenant who had not the experience to know when he was being fooled.

Losing over four hundred men to an ambush was not an option, so he turned abruptly on his heel and barked orders for moving out to his aide de camp.

The bugles sounded and men ran for their equipment. Officers shouted orders and the Fourth Regiment moved off toward the distant monolithic cliffs. A cloud of dust blurred the horizon as thousands of boots and hooves made their way west.

Setting the Stage(s)

Across the plains of the Llano, they stood like two sentinels guarding the high ground to the north. Their black granite shot from the flat ground over five hundred feet above the surroundings and formed peaks, one next to the other. The sky stretched for miles above and beyond the monoliths and they remained frozen in the blue, white-clouded setting of atmosphere and earth.

Double Mountain, as the place was called by the white man, was a link and landmark in the mostly featureless expanse of Eastern Texas, where the Comanche War Trail was.

The trail itself wove its way up from El Paso and careened across the red flatlands before turning around the two mountains and moving over the Caprock and across the Llano Estacado.

When the Comanche raided the Spanish settlements of the eighteenth century or the white of the nineteenth, they invariably passed these hills on their way to and from the destruction and mayhem wrought by their hands. Therefore, they held a special place in the hearts of the swift warriors of the Comanche. A certain comfort and familiarity was presented to the mind of the great tribe as these two mountains came into view. Excitement, freedom, and pride welled up and fought for dominion over the horse soldier when the two peaks came into view.

Such was the feeling that Quanah experienced as he neared the place. His brother Charlie was there on the side somewhere. He did not know the exact location, but he would soon find out.

Just then, a puff of smoke, as if in answer to his thought, rose above the prairie. There it was!

The blanket moved up and down across the smoldering fire, sending the message skyward. Charlie stepped back to admire his artfully created signal. It wouldn't be long before Quanah would join him and they would be able to bring their plans to fruition.

The only thing that was not assured, the one detail that irked more than the inherent uncertainty of war, was the heart of the woman. What Rebecca would do after the final escape remained to be seen.

Her love was available, yet somehow farther than it had ever been. She gave every signal of her positive intent, yet Charlie was never sure of himself in her presence and the aggressive aspects of his nature came to the forefront. It was a defense of sorts. He could not just roll over and let her control his actions. Therein lay the irony of the whole thing. Despite his attempts at not caring and pushing her away, his heart drew him nearer. Now he wanted to know. Was she his? He couldn't tell. He'd never experienced this before.

Shaking his head, Charlie descended the mountain to meet his brother.

Mackenzie peered once again through his glass. Folding his telescope, he frowned at the double mountain before him. Those two protrusions had caused more than one officer to lose his campaign. The Comanche were expert light cavalry, possibly the best the world had ever known. They would use the two hills as a redoubt to disappear behind and emerge unbeknownst to their pursuers in their rear. They used the formations with such devilish cunning that many an enemy had given up well before reaching the actual mountains.

Mackenzie knew his prey well and, more importantly, he knew his subordinate Dan would not stop to contemplate the situation but would rush in headlong.

There was no choice but to follow the trail where it led and hopefully be in a position to save the other half of his command if they met trouble.

Turning, he gave the order to march forward. The thin blue line formed and headed off amidst the dust and heat toward their fate.

Dan couldn't contain his glee. After sighting the smoke from the signal on Double Mountain and the dust from Mackenzie's troops approaching from the south, he knew his quarry was surrounded. There would be no escape, and a promotion for himself would surely follow!

He stretched and mounted his waiting horse with an athletic leap, swinging his leg over the saddle.

"Yah!" he shouted and dug his spurs into his horse's side, riding toward his troops and barking instructions for the attack.

A Stunning Turn of Events

Quanah emerged from the brush and made his way toward the outcropping of granite that stood like a sentry over the small valley between the two hills. There, standing atop the premonition like some spirit of the place, stood Charlie Bird. His arms akimbo, he looked toward his adopted brother and smiled.

"Come here, brother! Let us plan our final moves!"

Grinning back, Quanah said, "I'd like nothing better!"

They bowed their heads there in the wilds of western Texas and finalized what they hoped would be their escape and a lesson for the United States Army that subduing the Comanche would be no easy feat.

Mackenzie spurred his horse forward and looked down across the valley formed by the mountains. He shielded his eyes from the midday sun, which stood high overhead. A few shadows played over the rocky terrain. Blotches of gray broke the yellowish ground where rocks lay that had tumbled down the slopes.

Mosquitoes buzzed and a groundhog shuffled toward its lair. Other than those few movements, a perfect stillness was over the place. The wind did not stir and the air was bright and hot.

In an instant, his attention was focused on a splash of white cloth down below in the deepest part of the chasm separating the two hills. It was a dress! The wearer of the gown was, it appeared, a lady. At this distance, it was difficult to tell exactly who was there, but it was possible to discern that they were tied to a pole in the ground.

Instantly Mackenzie brought his field glass to his eye and looked again. Yes! It was the girl, head bowed and tied to stake fashioned from a piece of gnarled wood. At once something chivalrous sprang up in his breast. He must prevent the maiden from being harmed.

Caution flew to the wind.

"Men! Follow me!" he exclaimed and galloped down the slope, rocks and stones tumbling before him.

The entire corps followed their leader into the defile, pushing and shoving to get to the woman who was detained in so heinous a fashion at the bottom between the hills.

On the other side of the valley and at nearly the same instant, Dan beheld the same sight. A very similar feeling made its way into his heart. He could not let such an act go unpunished by these savages! First though, he had to save the girl. His men—from officer to private—felt the same way and poured over the edge of the hill in a torrent of manly heroics.

If one were to have looked upon this scene from above, the bird's-eye view, they would have witnessed a unique thing: two masses of blue rolling toward a single point in their front, converging with two horsemen in the lead, each riding at top speed to get there first.

Mackenzie succeeded in reaching the prisoner a hair's breath sooner and leapt from his horse. As the others watched in breathless expectation, the chief gently lifted the chin of the bound woman.

As her countenance was lifted to the sky, Mackenzie leapt back in surprise!

What was this? A mustache? A gasp echoed from all those close enough to see. Don Carlos, drunk as a skunk, grinned back at his savior, belched, and then passed out.

The Colonel's mouth fell open and he turned in astonishment toward the mountains above.

The peals of laughter rolled toward him at the realization that he and his entire command had been tricked.

Seconds of shock were followed by the thunderous crashing of boulders, jostled loose from their spots by cleverly placed sticks in the hills above. The dust rose up as the army's hope sank and in very little time the entire force became trapped.

Charlie sprang to the top of a particularly large boulder and shouted down, "Mackenzie, I'd shoot you where you are but the embarrassment you'll get from this will be worse than a bullet in your heart!"

Mackenzie raised his pistol to shoot but Charlie had vanished, although his laughter remained to taunt his former pursuers.

He leapt down and trotted toward his friends who were gathered at the foot of the taller hill.

Quanah stepped forward to embrace him.

"Charlie, we must run," he warned, but couldn't conceal a smile. "Ah! You planned it so well!" The bigger man tousled his brother's hair and shoved him playfully.

"I couldn't have done anything without your help!"

"Or without my old dress!" Rebecca called from atop Charlie's horse.

"Indeed! I had my doubts about your loyalties!"

"You needn't have worried," she spoke emotionally. A blush crossed her beautiful features. She did not move her eyes from Charlie.

A broad smile crept across his face as he mounted a horse that was being held by one of his men.

"We ride!" he motioned north and west with his hand and rode off. The others followed. The line of riders disappeared into the setting sun as the first of the blue soldiers scaled the peak.

Mackenzie glared after them and felt for his missing fingers.

A Peaceful End

The children sat in awe around Quanah and Charlie for nearly two hours as the stories poured forth. They finally finished when the chief motioned that he needed a rest.

The children rushed into the house in the late afternoon sun, starving for supper with Charlie following on their heels.

Just as he was about to enter the house, his brother called out to him, "Charlie! Know that although we are not of the same parents, we are brothers as sure as the moon rises every evening."

Charlie responded with a questioning glance, then embraced his brother and went into the house to eat.

The great chief surveyed his surroundings with pride, shut his eyes, then the cane fell from his hand. On that day, on the porch of the Star House, he joined his ancestors on the great hunting grounds.

Tales on the LLano Estacado

A Lesson in Buffalo Hunting

Lying in the grass wet with morning dew, the hunter scanned the horizon for a sign of the great herd.

Charlie looked over at his brother lying next to him and motioned in the direction of the rising sun. There, where the table land melted into the horizon, a faint cloud of dust began to form. Seeing it too, Quanah rose from a prone position and stretched his long limbs. All around him, other braves appeared from their resting spots in the tall grass.

"Charlie, get the horses! They will be upon us before too much longer."

The younger hunter ran to the edge of the clearing where the horses were tethered. He brought two, his own and his brother's, to the spot where they had been waiting. As they mounted, the excitement grew in all of them until it was like a living thing.

Bounding off in the direction of the ever-widening cloud kicked up by thousands of hooves, Charlie checked his rifle as he had been instructed by his brother lest it fail at an inopportune time, perhaps when being charged by a large bull, seething with anger at his antagonists. If he did not feel it secure, he was to return to the safety of the high pasture and let the others continue the hunt. Luckily, it tested true with a satisfying snap of the priming mechanism.

Galloping across the grassland, the ten horseman spread themselves out into a "V". The ground became harder and the grass shorter as they charged full speed towards the beasts that were just becoming visible in the distance.

The brown mass on the horizon separated into individual animals. They were bigger than a small wagon, covered in uneven fur, horns protruding 3 feet to either side of some.

Aside from their immense size, Charlie found their sheer number striking! From one end of the Llano Estado to the other, a sea of buffalo stretched for miles.

There it was! The lead Buffalo emerged from the great crowd of shaggy brown fur and ran full speed across the range. With surprising agility for it's immense size, it leaped over a small ravine in its path followed by the stronger members of the herd.

As if grabbed by some invisible hand, the hunters were drawn to this lead animal. They raced across the ground, all the while careful not to have their horses' hooves catch in one of the many prairie dog holes.

Finally, at a distance of fifty feet Quanah gave the signal, Charlie lifted his rifle to his shoulder and took careful aim. The rifle cracked and echoed against the distant cliffs.

The great lumbering beast leapt as the 50 caliber bullet ripped into its shoulder just below the neck. A spurt of dust lifted from the fur and the buffalo seemed to stumble momentarily. In an incredible show of energy, it then roared and took off in the direction of the men chasing it. The other bison followed suit. Soon, the hunters became the pursued.

Charlie's eyes widened in surprise as he spurred his horse in the opposite direction. He glanced over at Quanah, who although galloping at full tilt away from the stampede, kept looking over his shoulder.

Suddenly with a bellow, the lead buffalo tipped over, shuddered, and then lay still.

The warriors turned at the sound and watched the animal plow into the ground. Then, the most amazing thing happened. Charlie expected the other bison to continue in pursuit but they gathered about their dead leader, milling about in a confused state.

The hunters immediately began firing into the confused mass of animals, dropping ten of them and then stopping. More than enough had been killed for the tribe.

After few moments, a large male buffalo emerged from the herd and trotted off in the opposite direction. The others followed until the only remaining objects on the field were the Comanche hunters and the downed buffalo.

Charlie looked to his older brother with abject admiration at the workmanlike way in which the buffalo had been hunted.

"Now what?" asked the younger man.

In response, Quanah unsheathed the knife from his saddle and tossed it to Charlie.

With a smile turning to his horse he said, "Now you butcher them. We'll see you back at the camp."

Goodbye Mother

Shaken suddenly from sleep, she perceived a dim shadow pass across her field of vision. Then it was gone. She was awake again.

How many days had it been? She could not recall. The days and nights melted into a single piece. Time passed and she sank into delirium. The woman could not be sure whether she was awake or dreaming. Often she was hot, so hot that had she the strength she would have hurled the blanket from her person. Other periods passed where she was so cold that she shivered until the blanket would fall off. In would rush the nurse to restore it, but it did little to offer any succor. Now, thankfully all this had passed and she was merely numb. The end would be coming soon.

The darkened room was in a house belonging to a man called Goodnight, one of her "saviors". He was of the troop who had ambushed the sleeping Indians 10 years earlier and destroyed her life.

They had many attempts to "civilize" her. To bring back from the savagery of her younger years. It had not worked. She had resisted it at every step. She would not speak their language. She would not dress in their clothes, nor sleep in their beds. She much preferred to sleep on the ground with only a blanket as her mattress.

Worse, her daughter, the Flower of the Prairie, had been taken to be raised in an orphanage until such a time when her mother would be able to take care of her as a white woman "should."

Now, her life was passing in the shadows.

The apparition appeared again and she attempted to call out. If for no other reason than her wanting to demonstrate that she was still alive.

A strong brown hand reached out and grasped the withered hand there on the yellow blanket. There were times, not long past, that the hand was strong, full of energy. It had raised three children and skinned many a bison. Now it was nearly lifeless, much like the body it was attached to.

"Mother," the deep voice called out softly in the Comanche dialect.

Cynthia Parker started and looked to her left.

"Quanah! Is that you? My son?"

"Yes," the big chief said, suppressing a sob. "Yes it is, mother. I have come to be with you now in your time of trouble. The Great Spirit will be with you!"

"I worry not for myself. But you must flee! If they catch you here in Texas they will kill you!"

"I have no fear of them. They shall not catch me. When I heard you were sick I came as soon as possible. How do you feel?"

"My time is done," she said, speaking resignedly. Then, with as much force as she could muster, she added, "I care only for you, my younger son, and my sweet daughter!"
The warrior fell silent.
"Does your silence bode ill for them? Please tell me they live!"

Quanah struggled with his response, finally saying, "I know not about our sister but *my* brother fairs well! He has become a great warrior!" he spoke referring to Charlie.

"It is well," she sighed. She then smiled up at the handsome face and closed her eyes for the last time.

As the hand went limp in his grasp, Quanah sunk his head on the blanket and then with a resolute motion rose and kissed his mother's brow. Covering her head with a blanket, he began to weep.

The noise brought the house running to the sickroom but when they opened the door, the room was empty save for the body and one feather atop the bed cover.

A maiden picked it up and wondered who had been there in that dark room.

The Deadeye Kid Meets Charlie Bird

Charlie reigned up in front of the field. To his right was the broad, shallow river, sparkling in the morning light. To his left the great grasslands stretching south as far as the eye could see, dotted here and there with Joshua trees. In front lay the otherworldly peaks of the Rockies, jutting like great purple sentinels, guarding the West from encroachment of man.

Of course, there were many ways to cross them and the riches of the mountainous spine of the country were already being exploited. In those early days, man's imagination had not yet fathomed settling the Rockies and they still captured the imagination with their abject grandeur.

Rebecca, whose horse had been picking its way along the river trail, halted her mare next to Charlie's.

"Can we cross them? "she wondered. "It looks impossible."

Charlie Bird turned to her, "I'm surprised to hear you say that," he said with a mischievous grin crossing his features. "You, of all people, should know that nothing is impossible.

Charlie and Rebecca were hardly the only humans on the desolate plain. A pair of eyes, one white and glassy, the other deep brown, appeared above a dip in the ground and watched the riders. He had been tracking a deer that had run out of the woods when the pair had appeared from the trail running along the river. He had had just enough time to lie down and so conceal himself.

The couple were looking toward the distant mountains and talking, although being beyond earshot, what they said was impossible to discern. Whatever it was they were talking about was immaterial. Those packs that hung from the saddles seemed bursting with just the type of things an outlaw on the run might kill for.

Ronald J. Turnbridge, known in the newspapers and among the cattlemen of the country as the "Deadeye Kid", not for his uncanny ability to pick off targets at a distance but because of his youthful appearance and the dead-white right eye that he declined to conceal. The injury, a relic of a particularly brutal bar fight when he was eighteen, was sported as one might wear a badge of honor. It increased his credibility as an all-out fighter who would not let something as small as an eye get in the way of defeating his enemies.

The Deadeye Kid had no intention of letting these two live but he might as well have a little fun with them instead of just shooting them both in the back. There was also a chance that, regardless of how fast he was, you never knew who you were dealing with. The man, who looked like a curious cross between a white man and an Indian, might get off a shot even after he'd been hit. Better to disarm them first. They also might have some info about a posse or two that was on his trail. Worth it to find out by asking directly.

With these three reasons in mind, the kid rose from his hiding place and called out to the two riders.

Charlie had been alerted to the presence of another some minutes ago. He knew not whether the wind shifted or that his senses had been honed to such a point that he was more aware than a usual person. Whatever the reason, he detected something and was prepared. Upon hearing someone hail them from behind, Rebecca started but Charlie Bird casually turned in the saddle in the direction of the call.

"Hey there, pardner!" the man was yelling as he ambled in their direction. "I just need a bit of news. Do you know if there's a well 'round these parts?"

Something in the Kid's manner put Charlie on high alert and he didn't respond with words. Instead, he circled in front of Rebecca to shield her.

The Deadeye Kid stopped ten feet from the riders and shoved his hands in his jean pockets.

"I'm kinder thirsty you know," he spoke casually looking out from beneath the brim of his wide brimmed black hat. "If'n you got some water to spare or knows where a well might be, I'd be much obliged."

"I don't know of any," Charlie responded in a soft voice. "It's certainly odd for you to just be wandering around here. It's pretty desolate."

"Don't I knows it! There's some fellers out there that want to have a word or two with me about some land they claim is theirs but I knows is mine by right! My grandaddy left it to me and they wants to steal it from me. You didn't hear about anything 'bout that, did you? Like maybe a posse?"

"Well, I don't think we have. I'm sorry, we don't know about water or have any to spare. We'll just be getting along now."

A pistol appeared in the Deadeye Kid's right hand in an instant.

"I don't think you'll be getting along nowheres too quick now," the Kid spoke coolly.

"Charlie!" Rebecca screamed as the shot rang out.

The Deadeye Kid looked up in surprise from the web of blood spreading across his chest and toppled over in a heap.

Charlie holstered his pistol and grabbed Rebecca's nervous horse in one motion.

"Oh my!" she said, her voice trembling slightly. "I didn't even see you pull out your gun!"

"Well, I didn't think it would be a good idea to have it out when he came up on us. Might make him nervous. As it was, he looked away for a little too long and I just pulled and got him. Now, please watch the horses while I drag him over to the woods and bury him. If anyone finds him out here, they might follow us."

Twenty minutes later they rode out of the clearing and into the wild mountains, Rebecca having found yet another thing to marvel at in Charlie.

Retrieval

The Adobe Hut was the only man-made structure for miles. It sat like an old, yellow tooth protruding from the maw that was the valley below his feet.

Twice he called out with no response, checking to make sure it was abandoned before he tied his horse to a stunted Joshua tree, and walked down the rocky path.

A high Western sun beat down fiercely on his shoulders. The old, worn boots he wore crunched on the dry stones; how long had it been since it had rained? He hoped the old well hadn't gone dry or this would be an uncomfortable stay.

The sack he carried made him stagger at times. The old greasy burlap bag was weighted with good old banknotes numbering in the thousands, so he guessed it was worth the trouble. A few weeks of hiding out and he'd be able to show his face again in some California town and spend money like a king and no one would be the wiser. For now, he'd lay low.

As he approached the hut, he paused and knelt to see if anyone had passed that way. Seeing nothing, he approached the rudely cut doorway and peered inside.

There was an ancient, dusty bed, a table with a wooden chair and some crude utensils. A large, black pot hung on the opposite wall. A layer of dust over it all spoke of its lengthy vacant state.

"Hello!" Dirk Stangerson called.

He was answered by his own voice echoing off the smooth walls.

"Well, I guess we'll call this home for a while!" he grunted as he sat down on the cot.

The sack dropped at his feet, kicking up dust that set him coughing.

"Well there's no harm in counting again," he said struggling with the string that held the bag shut.

Suddenly the room darkened as the opening was eclipsed by a huge figure, black silhouette moving swiftly into the room.

"Q..Quanah?" Stangerson sputtered, feeling his mouth go dry. "How did you find me?"

In answer Quanah grabbed the skinny cowboy's throat and lifted him bodily from the bed. His hat fell to the floor and rolled to a far corner.

"You think you steal from Comanche people and just walk away?" the big Indian spat through clenched teeth.

Stangerson could only reply with a gurgle as he struggled to breath, eyes rolling back in his head.

"I think you know you never escape! I think maybe we just leave you to buzzards," and with that Quanah tightened his grip such that the thief's eyes bulged from the sockets and his face turned a sickly shade of purple.

Releasing his grip, the big native let Stangerson drop to the wooden floorboards with a sickening thud.

Quanah bent to the sack and heaved it over his shoulders. Even to the warrior chief, the bag seemed heavy. The contents were to sustain the tribe for the winter and this rogue contractor was attempting make off with it all!

Stangerson had regained his breath and sat himself gingerly on the mattress. His countenance bore the expression of one who had looked over the precipice of death and had barely returned.

Quanah waited until the heavy gasping of his opponent subsided before speaking.

"Look at me! You think I will let you starve my people? You think you just get away? Tell me why I not kill you now?"

"Oh no! I was not running away!" the man pleaded, falling to his knees. "I was keeping the money safe! Black Jake wanted it! I took it to hide it from him!"

"I not believe you!"

"Oh, but you must! How can I prove it?" he pleaded from his knees, hands grasped in front.

Suddenly, an idea popped into the lanky man's scheming brain. He grinned a slimy grin and looked up at the big warrior.

"Say, Quanah, why don't we split it? You take half and I'll take the other and we'll both have more money than we can shake a stick at!"

A pleasant thought seemed to pass across the chief's mind which made him smile. Stangerson's heart leapt in hopes that his plea had some favor.

"Take off your boots and give me your pistol!" Quanah ordered quietly.

"Wh...What?"

"Boots and gun! Now!" he ordered again with more emphasis.

"Wha..Why?"

"You not hear me? Maybe I break your foot off instead?"

The contractor hurriedly removed his boots, holding them in his hand. With the other hand he removed his pistol and held it by the barrel so the warrior chief wouldn't get any wrong ideas.

"Give them to me!"

He stretched his hand forward and handed them to Quanah.

"Thanks!" he exclaimed. The chief about-faced and marched out of the hut.

"Where are you going with my boots?" came the plaintive call from the doorway.

No answer was forthcoming as he made his way up to the top of the valley where the thief's horse had been tethered.

"What are you doing?" Stangerson called out again, the fear welling up inside him.

Again, no answer.

Upon reaching the animal, Quanah calmly untied it and lead it towards his own waiting horse. Mounting his mare, he tugged on the other's leader and began trotting away.

Stangerson came charging out of the hovel yelling, "If you leave me here with no boots, no gun and no horse, I'll be a dead man! I won't last two days!"

The chief turned his horse and smiled wryly at the man.

"You care of that while women and children starve because you take their money to buy food? They freeze in the plains without this money to buy clothing! This you can accept and still think I feel bad you not survive?"

Stangerson's mouth dropped open.

"But you can't just leave me here!"

Quanah grinned back at him and turned away. The ride back to the reservation was long but satisfying.

Historical Note:

One thing I enjoy most about reading historical fiction is trying to figure out what is real and what is the product of the author's imagination. I know that I am not alone in this desire, so I have penned this little note in order to satisfy an inquisitive reader's curiosity.

Charlie Bird is first and foremost a work of fiction. Charlie did not exist and is the product of my own fancy. I did however base the idea on such real accounts as "Nine Years Among The Indians[1]". Apparently, the Comanche had fertility issues due their harsh lifestyle and nomadic proclivities. To fill their ranks, they would take in pre-adolescent captives and indoctrinate them in the tribal ways. Some, as was the case with Herman Lehmann (see above referenced book), fully embraced their new identity and did not willingly return to white society. It was but a small leap to create a character like Charlie Bird whose persona, although based on real possibilities, was really a product of my own experiences and feelings. The last part of the equation was to associate him with the towering personality of the real life last great chief of the Comanche.

Rebecca and her story were, to paraphrase the fictional Dr. John H. Watson in Nicholas Meyer's brilliant "Seven Percent Solution", made from whole cloth. It just seemed like the right character to provide a tough yet compassionate counter to Charlie's wild and daring nature.

---

[1] One can read the full book online here:
https://www.goodreads.com/book/show/147112.Nine_Years_Among_the_Indians_1870_1879

The Comanche Empire was real, or course. So too was Quanah Parker, their last great Chief. He finally came into the reservation in 1875 after a prolonged fight with the U.S. Army's Fourth Cavalry headed by the very real Colonel Ranald S. Mackenzie, or Bad Hand as referred to by his Native antagonists. Mackenzie did really lose a few fingers at the battle of Jerusalem Plank Road during the American Civil War.

The tale of the miners is completely fictional although there certainly could have been hunters for old Spanish silver in the Oklahoma hills.

Adobe walls was part of the Red River War[2] and occurred although not exactly as I've told it. Billy Dixson did make a shot that is still commemorated to this day.

The Battle at the end of the Mackenzie Triumphant story is very loosely based on the battle of Palo Duro Canyon on September 28th, 1874. Over 1500 horses were destroyed which constituted the main source of Comanche wealth. This was the last battle of any organized force of Comanche before they gave it all up and headed to the reservation.

Quanah died in 1911 at the Star House in Cache, Oklahoma. His mother's name really was Cynthia Parker and she was captured as a child during the Fort Parker Massacre in 1838. She had three children with Peta Nocona, Quanah's father and the Prologue is based on the Pease River Massacre[3].

To round everything out I'll just relate a few more bits and pieces. Little Wing was not a real person. Her name came from one of my favorite Jimi Hendrix songs. Don Carlos didn't exist either but was a fun character to invent for the story. So too Lieutenant Dan, who just might borrow his name from a famous movie.

---

[2] See: http://www.okhistory.org/publications/enc/entry.php?entry=RE010

[3] See: http://www.forttours.com/pages/pease.asp

If there is anything else I've left off, please accept my apologies.

Please feel free to email me at wevans915@gmail.com with any questions you have, and I'll do my best to answer them ☺

William Evans
Cleveland, Ohio – 2017

www.ingramcontent.com/pod-product-compliance
Lightning Source LLC
Chambersburg PA
CBHW020406150626
46554CB00012B/325